# FIVE GO TO MYSTERY MOOR

# FIVE GO TO
# MYSTERY MOOR

## ENID BLYTON

**Hodder
Children's
Books**

a division of Hodder Headline Limited

First published in Great Britain in 1954
by Hodder and Stoughton

This edition 2004
For sale in Indian Subcontinent only

For further information on Enid Blyton
please contact www.blyton.com

**27**

A catalogue record for this title
is available from the British Library

ISBN 0 340 89466 0

Typeset by Hewer Text Ltd, Edinburgh
Printed and bound in India by
Gopsons Papers Ltd., Noida

Hodder Children's Books
a division of Hodder Headline Limited
338 Euston Road
London NW1 3BH

# Contents

# [1]

## At the stables

'We've been here a week and I've been bored every single minute!' said George.

'You haven't,' said Anne. 'You've enjoyed all the rides we've had, and you know you've enjoyed messing about the stables when we haven't been out riding.'

'I tell you, I've been bored every single *minute*,' said George, quite fiercely. 'I ought to know, oughtn't I? That awful girl Henrietta too. Why do we have to put up with her?'

'Oh – Henry!' said Anne, with a laugh. 'I should have thought you'd find a lot in common with another girl like yourself, who would rather be a boy, and tries to act like one!'

The two girls were lying by a haystack eating sandwiches. Round them in a field were many horses, most of which the girls either rode or looked after. Some way off was an old rambling building, and by the front entrance was a great board,

### Captain Johnson's Riding School

Anne and George had been staying there for a week, while Julian and Dick had gone to camp with other boys from their school. It had been Anne's idea. She was fond of horses, and had heard so much from her friends at school what fun it was to spend day after day at the stables, that she had made up her mind to go herself.

George hadn't wanted to come. She was sulky because the two boys had gone off somewhere without her and Anne, for a change. Gone to camp! George would have liked that, but girls were not allowed to go camping with the boys from Julian's school, of course. It was a camp just for the boys alone.

'You're silly to keep feeling cross because you couldn't go camping too,' said Anne. 'The boys don't want us girls round them all the time.'

George thought differently. 'Why not? I can do anything that Dick and Julian can do,' she said. 'I can climb, and bike for miles, I can walk as far as they can, I can swim, I can beat a whole lot of boys at most things.'

'That's what Henry says!' said Anne, with a laugh. 'Look, there she is, striding about as usual, hands in her jodhpur pockets, whistling like the stable boy!'

George scowled. Anne had been very much amused to see how Henrietta and George hated one another at sight – and yet both had so very much the same ideas. George's real name was Georgina, but she would only answer to George. Henry's real name was Henrietta, but she would only answer to Henry, or Harry to her *very* best friends!

She was about as old as George, and her hair was short too, but it wasn't curly. 'It's a pity yours is curly,' she said to George, pityingly. 'It looks so *girlish*, doesn't it?'

'Don't be an ass,' George said, curtly. 'Plenty of boys have curly hair.'

The maddening part was that Henrietta was a wonderful rider, and had won all kinds of cups. George hadn't enjoyed herself a bit during that week at the stables, because for once another girl had outshone her. She couldn't bear to see Henrietta striding about, whistling, doing everything so competently and quickly.

Anne had had many a quiet laugh to herself, especially when the two girls had each made up their minds not to call one another Henry and George, but to use their full names, Henrietta and Georgina! This meant that neither of them would answer the other when called, and Captain Johnson, the big burly owner of the riding stables, got very tired of both of them.

'What are you behaving like this for?' he demanded one morning, seeing their sulky looks at one another at breakfast-time. 'Behaving like a couple of idiotic schoolgirls!'

That made Anne laugh! A couple of idiotic school*girls*. My goodness, how annoyed both girls were with Captain Johnson. Anne was a bit scared of him. He was hot-tempered, outspoken, and stood no nonsense at all, but he was a wonder with the horses, and loved a good, hearty laugh. He and his wife took either boys or girls for the holidays, and worked them hard, but the children always enjoyed their stay immensely.

'If it hadn't been for Henry, you'd have been perfectly happy this week,' said Anne, leaning back against the haystack. 'We've had heavenly April weather, the horses are lovely, and I like Captain and Mrs Johnson very much.'

'I wish the boys were here,' said George. 'They would soon put that silly Henrietta in her place. I wish I'd stayed at home now.'

'Well, you had the choice,' said Anne, rather cross. 'You could have stayed at Kirrin Cottage with your father and mother, but you chose to come here with me, till the boys came back from camp. You shouldn't make such a fuss if things aren't exactly to your liking. It spoils things for *me*.'

'Sorry,' said George. 'I'm being a pig, I know, but I do miss the boys. We can only be with

them in the hols and it seems funny without
them. There's just *one* thing that pleases me
here, you'll be glad to know . . .'

'You needn't tell me, I know what it is!' said
Anne, with a laugh. 'You're glad that Timmy
won't have anything to do with Henry!'

'With Henrietta,' corrected George. She
grinned suddenly. 'Yes, old Timmy's got some
sense. He just can't stick her. Here, Timmy boy,
leave those rabbit holes alone and come and lie
down for a bit. You've run for miles this
morning when we took the horses out, and
you've snuffled down about a hundred rabbit
holes. Come and be peaceful.'

Timmy left his latest rabbit hole reluctantly
and came to flop down beside Anne and
George. He gave George a hearty lick and
she patted him.

'We're just saying, Timmy, how sensible you
are not to make friends with that awful Henrietta,' said George. She stopped suddenly at a
sharp nudge from Anne. A shadow fell across
them as someone came round the haystack.

It was Henrietta. By the annoyed look on her face it was clear that she had heard George's remark. She held out an envelope to George.

'A letter for you, Georgina,' she said, stiffly. 'I thought I'd better bring it in case it was important.'

'Oh, thanks, Henrietta,' said George, and took the envelope. She tore it open, read it and groaned.

'Look at that!' she said to Anne and passed it to her. 'It's from Mother.'

Anne took the letter and read it. 'Please stay another week. Your father is not well. Love from Mother.'

'What bad luck!' said George, a familiar scowl on her face. 'Just when I thought we'd be going home in a day or two, and the boys would join us at Kirrin. Now we'll be stuck here by ourselves for ages! What's the matter with Father? I bet he's only got a headache or something, and doesn't want us stamping about in and out of the house and making a noise.'

'We could go to *my* home,' said Anne. 'That's

if you don't mind its being a bit upside-down because of the decorating we're having done.'

'No. I know you want to stay here with the horses,' said George. 'Anyway your father and mother are abroad, we'd only be in the way. Blow, blow, blow! Now we'll have to do without the boys for another week. They'll stay on in camp, of course.'

Captain Johnson said yes, certainly the two girls could stay on. It was possible that they might have to do a bit of camping out if one or two extra children came, but they wouldn't mind that, would they?

'Not a bit,' said George. 'Actually we'd rather like to be on our own, Anne and I. We've got Timmy, you see. So long as we could come in to meals and do a few jobs for you, we'd love to go off on our own.'

Anne smiled to herself. What George really meant was that she wanted to see as little of Henrietta as possible! Still, it *would* be fun to camp out if the weather was fine. They could easily borrow a tent from Captain Johnson.

'Bad luck, Georgina!' said Henry, who was listening to all this. 'Very bad luck! I know you're terribly bored here. It's a pity you don't really like horses. It's a pity that you—'

'Shut up,' said George, rudely, and went out of the room. Captain Johnson glared at Henrietta, who stood whistling at the window, hands in pockets.

'You two girls!' he said. 'Why don't you behave yourselves? Always aping the boys, pretending you're so mannish! Give me Anne here, any day! What you want is your ears boxing. Did you take that bale of straw to the stables?'

'Yes,' said Henrietta, without turning.

Suddenly, a small boy came running in. 'There's a traveller kid outside with a horse, a skewbald, a mangy-looking thing. He says can you help him – the horse has got something wrong with its leg.'

'Those travellers again!' said Captain Johnson. 'All right, I'll come.'

He went out and Anne went with him, not

wanting to be left alone with the angry Henrietta. She found George outside with a traveller boy and a patient little skewbald horse, its brown and white coat looking very flea-bitten.

'What have you done to your horse *this* time?' said Captain Johnson, looking at its leg. 'You'll have to leave it here, and I'll see to it.'

'I can't do that,' said the boy. 'We're off to Mystery Moor again.'

'Well, you'll have to,' said Captain Johnson. 'It's not fit to walk. Your caravan can't go with the others, this horse isn't fit to pull it. I'll get the police to your father if you try to work this horse before it's better.'

'Don't do that!' said the boy. 'It's just that my dad says we've *got* to go tomorrow.'

'What's the hurry?' said Captain Johnson. 'Can't your caravan wait a day or two? Mystery Moor will still be there in two days' time! It beats me why you go there, a desolate place like that, not even a farm or cottage for miles!'

'I'll leave the horse,' said the boy, and

stroked the skewbald's nose. It was clear that he loved the ugly little horse. 'My father will be angry, but the other caravans can go on without us. We'll have to catch them up.'

He gave a kind of half-salute to the captain and disappeared from the stable-yard, a skinny little sunburnt figure. The skewbald stood patiently.

'Take it round to the small stable,' said Captain Johnson to George and Anne. 'I'll come and see to it in a minute.'

The girls led the little horse away. 'Mystery Moor!' said George. 'What an odd name! The boys would like that, they'd be exploring it at once, wouldn't they?'

'Yes. I do wish they were coming here,' said Anne. 'Still, I expect they'll like the chance of staying on in camp. Come on, you funny little creature, here's the stable!'

The girls shut the door on the traveller's pony and turned to go back. William, the boy who had brought the message about the horse, yelled to them.

'Hey, George and Anne! There's *another* letter for you!'

The two hurried into the house at once. 'Oh, I hope Father is better and we can go home and join the boys at Kirrin!' said George. She tore open the envelope and then gave a yell that made Anne jump.

'Look, see what it says. They're coming *here*!' Anne snatched the letter and read it.

'Joining you tomorrow. We'll camp out if no room. Hope you've got a nice juicy adventure ready for us! Julian and Dick.'

'They're coming! They're coming!' said Anne, as excited as George. '*Now* we'll have some fun!'

'It's a pity we've no adventure to offer them,' said George. 'Still, you simply never know!'

# *[2]*

# *Julian, Dick – and Henry*

George was quite a different person now that she knew her two cousins were coming the next day. She was even polite to Henrietta!

Captain Johnson scratched his head when he heard that the boys were arriving. 'We can't have them in the house, except for meals,' he said. 'We're full up. They can either sleep in the stables or have a tent. I don't care which.'

'There will be ten altogether then,' said his wife. 'Julian, Dick, Anne, George, Henry – and John, Susan, Alice, Rita and William. Henry may have to camp out too.'

'Not with us,' said George, at once.

'I think you're rather unkind to Henry,' said Mrs Johnson. 'After all, you and she are very alike, George. You both think you ought to have been boys, and—'

'I'm not a *bit* like Henrietta!' said George, indignantly. 'You wait till my cousins come, Mrs Johnson. *They* won't think she's like me. I don't expect they'll want anything to do with her.'

'Oh well, you'll just have to shake down together somehow, if you want to stay here,' said Mrs Johnson. 'Let me see, I'd better get some rugs out. The boys will want them, whether they sleep in the stables or in a tent. Come and help me to look for them, Anne.'

Anne, George and Henry were a good bit older than the other five children staying at the stables, but all of them, small or big, were excited to hear about the coming of Julian and Dick. For one thing George and Anne had related so many of the adventures they had had with them, that everyone was inclined to think of them as heroes.

Henrietta disappeared after tea that day and could not be found. 'Wherever have you been?' demanded Mrs Johnson when she at last turned up.

'Up in my room,' said Henrietta. 'Cleaning my shoes and my jods, and mending my riding jacket. You keep telling me to, and now I've done it!'

'Aha! Preparing for the heroes!' said Captain Johnson, and Henry immediately put on a scowl very like the one George often wore.

'Nothing of the sort!' she said. 'I've been meaning to do it for a long time. If Georgina's cousins are anything like *her* I shan't be very interested in them.'

'But you might like my brothers,' said Anne, with a laugh. 'If you don't there'll be something wrong with you.'

'Don't be silly,' said Henrietta. 'Georgina's cousins and your brothers are the same people!'

'How clever of you to work that out,' said George. But she felt too happy to keep up the silly bickering for long. She went out with Timmy, whistling softly.

'They're coming tomorrow, Tim,' she said. 'Julian and Dick. We'll all go off together, like we always do, the five of us. You'll like that, won't you, Timmy?'

'Woof,' said Timmy approvingly and waved his plumy tail. He knew quite well what she meant.

Next morning George and Anne looked up the trains that arrived at the station two miles away. 'This is the one they'll come by,' said George, her finger on the timetable. 'It's the only one this morning. It arrives at half past twelve. We'll go and meet them.'

'Right,' said Anne. 'We'll start at ten minutes to twelve – we'll be in plenty of time then. We can help them with their things. They won't bring much.'

'Take the ponies up to Hawthorn Field, will you?' called Captain Johnson. 'Can you manage all four of them?'

'Oh yes,' said Anne, pleased. She loved the walk to Hawthorn Field, up a little narrow lane set with celandines, violets and primroses, and the fresh green of the budding hawthorn bushes. 'Come on, George. Let's catch the ponies and take them now. It's a heavenly morning.'

They set off with the four frisky ponies, Timmy at their heels. He was quite a help with the horses at the stable, especially when any had to be caught.

No sooner had they left the stables and gone on their way to Hawthorn Field than the telephone rang. It was for Anne.

'Oh, I'm sorry, she's not here,' said Mrs Johnson, answering it. 'Who is it speaking? Oh, Julian her brother? Can I give her a message?'

'Yes, please,' said Julian's voice. 'Tell her we are arriving at the bus-stop at Milling Green at half past eleven, and is there a little hand-cart she and George could bring, because we've got our tent with us and other odds and ends?'

'Oh, we'll send the little wagon,' said Mrs Johnson. 'The one that always goes to meet the train or the bus. I'll get George to meet you with Anne, they can drive it in. We're pleased you are coming. The weather's very good and you'll enjoy yourselves!'

'You bet!' said Julian. 'Thanks awfully for

putting us up. We won't be any trouble, in fact we'll help all we can.'

Mrs Johnson said good-bye and put down the receiver. She saw Henrietta passing outside the window, looking much cleaner and tidier than usual. She called to her.

'Henry! Where are George and Anne? Julian and Dick are arriving at the bus-stop at Milling Green at eleven thirty and I've said we'll meet them in the little wagon. Will you tell George and Anne? They can put Winkie into the cart and trot him down to the bus-stop.'

'Right,' said Henry. Then she remembered that George and Anne had been sent up to Hawthorn Field with four ponies.

'I say, they won't be back in time!' she called. 'Shall *I* take the wagon and meet them?'

'Yes, do. That would be kind of you, Henry,' said Mrs Johnson. 'You'd better hurry, though. Time's getting on. Where's Winkie? In the big field?'

'Yes,' said Henry and hurried off to get him. Soon he was in the wagon shafts, and Henry was in the driving-seat. She drove off smartly, grinning to herself to think how cross George and Anne would be to find they had missed meeting the two boys after all.

Julian and Dick had already arrived at the bus-stop when Henry drove up. They looked hopefully at the wagon, thinking that perhaps one of the girls was driving in to meet them.

'No go,' said Dick. 'It's somebody else, driving into the village. I wonder if the girls got our message. I thought they would meet us at the bus-stop here. Well, we'll wait a few minutes more.'

They had just sat down on the bus-stop seat again when the wagon stopped nearby. Henry saluted them.

'Are you Anne's brothers?' she called. 'She didn't get your telephone message, so I've come with the wagon instead. Get in!'

'Oh, jolly nice of you,' said Julian, dragging his things to the wagon. 'Er – I'm Julian – and this is Dick. What's your name?'

'Henry,' said Henrietta, helping Julian with

his things. She heaved them in valiantly, then
clicked to Winkie to stand still and not fidget.
'I'm glad you've come. There are rather a lot of
small kids at the stables. We'll be glad of you
two! I say, Timmy will be pleased to see you,
won't he?'

'Good old Tim,' said Dick, heaving his things
in. Henry gave them a shove too. She wasn't
very fat but she was wiry and strong. She
grinned round at the boys. 'All set! Now we'll
get back to the stables. Or do you want to have
an ice-cream or anything before we start? Din-
ner's not till one.'

'No. We'll get on, I think,' said Julian. Henry
leapt into the driver's seat, took the reins and
clicked to Winkie. The boys were behind in the
wagon. Winkie set off at a spanking pace.

'Nice boy!' said Dick to Julian, in a low
voice, as they drove off. 'Decent of him to meet
us.'

Julian nodded. He was disappointed that
Anne and George hadn't come with Timmy,
but it was good to be met by *someone*! It

wouldn't have been very funny to walk the long road to the farm carrying their packs by themselves.

They arrived at the stables and Henry helped them down with their things. Mrs Johnson heard them arriving and came to the door to welcome them.

'Ah, there you are. Come along in. I've a mid-morning snack for you, because I guessed you'd have had breakfast early. Leave the things there, Henry. If the boys sleep in one of the stables, there's no sense in bringing them into the house. Now, are George and Anne still not back? What a pity!'

Henry disappeared to put away the wagon. The boys went into the pleasant house and sat down to lemonade and home-made biscuits. They had hardly taken a bite before Anne came running in. 'Henry told me you'd come! Oh, I'm sorry we didn't meet you! We thought you'd come by train!'

Timmy came racing in, his tail waving madly. He leapt at the two boys, who were just giving Anne a hug each. Then in came George, her face one big beam.

'Julian! Dick! I *am* so glad you've come! It's been dull as ditch-water without you! Did anyone meet you?'

'Yes. An awfully nice boy,' said Dick. 'Gave us quite a welcome and dragged our packs into the wagon, and was very friendly. You never told us about him.'

'Oh, was that William?' said Anne. 'Well, he's only little. We didn't bother about telling you of the juniors here.'

'No, he wasn't little,' said Dick. 'He was quite big, very strong too. You didn't mention him at all.'

'Well, we told you about the other *girl* here,' said George. 'Henrietta, awful creature! Thinks she's like a boy and goes whistling about everywhere. She makes us laugh! You'll laugh too.'

A sudden thought struck Anne. 'Did the – er – boy who met you, tell you his name?' she asked.

'Yes, what was it now, Henry,' said Dick. 'Nice chap. I'm going to like him.'

George stared as if she couldn't believe her ears. '*Henry*! Did *she* meet you?'

'No – not she – *he*,' corrected Julian. 'Fellow with a big grin.'

'But that's *Henrietta*!' cried George, her face flaming red with anger. 'The awful girl I told you about, who tries to act like a boy, and whistles and strides about all over the place. Don't tell me she took you in! She calls herself Henry, instead of Henrietta, and wears her hair short, and—'

'Gosh, she sounds very like *you*, George,' said Dick. 'Well, I never! It never occurred to me that he was a girl. Jolly good show she put up. I must say I liked him – her, I mean.'

'*Oh*!' said George, really furious. 'The beast! She goes and meets you and never says a word to us, and makes you think she's a boy – and – and – spoils everything!'

'Hold your horses, George, old thing,' said Julian, surprised. 'After all, you've often been pleased when people take *you* for a boy, though goodness knows why. I thought you'd grown out of it a bit. Don't blame us for thinking Henry was a boy, and liking him – her, I mean.'

George stamped out of the room. Julian scratched his head and looked at Dick. 'Now we've put our foot in it,' he said. 'What an ass George is! I should have thought she'd have liked someone like Henry, who had exactly the same ideas as she has. Well, she'll get over it, I suppose.'

'It's going to be a bit awkward,' said Anne, soberly.

She was right. It was going to be *very* awkward!

# [3]

## Sniffer

As soon as George had gone out of the room, a scowl on her face, Henry walked in, hands in jodhpur pockets.

'Hallo!' said Dick, at once. '*Henrietta*!'

Henry grinned. 'Oh, so they've told you, have they? I was tickled pink when you took me for a boy.'

'You've even got your riding jacket buttons buttoning up the wrong way,' said Anne, noticing for the first time. 'You really are an idiot, Henry. You and George are a pair!'

'Well, I look more like a real boy than George does, anyway,' said Henry.

'Only because of your hair,' said Dick. 'It's straight.'

'Don't say that in front of George,' said

Anne. 'She'll immediately have hers cut like a convict or something, all shaven and shorn.'

'Well, anyway, it was jolly decent of Henry to come and meet us and lug our things about,' said Julian. 'Have a biscuit, anyone?'

'No thanks,' said Anne and Henry.

'Are we supposed to leave any for politeness' sake?' said Dick, eyeing the plate. 'They're home-made and quite super. I could wolf the lot.'

'We aren't especially polite here,' said Henry, with a grin. 'We aren't especially clean and tidy, either. We have to change out of our jods at night for supper, which is an awful nuisance, especially as Captain Johnson never bothers to change his.'

'Any news?' asked Julian, drinking the last of the lemonade. 'Anything exciting happened?'

'No, nothing,' said Anne. 'The only excitement is the horses, nothing more. This is quite a lonely place, really, and the only exciting thing we've heard is the name of the big, desolate moor that stretches from here to the coast. Mystery Moor it's called.'

'Why?' asked Dick. 'Some long-ago mystery gave it that name, I suppose?'

'I don't know,' said Anne. 'I think only travellers go there now. A little traveller boy came in with a lame horse yesterday, and said his people had to go to Mystery Moor. Why they wanted to go to such a deserted stretch of land I don't know – no farms there, not even a cottage.'

'Travellers have peculiar ideas sometimes,' said Henry. 'I must say I like the way they leave messages for any traveller following – patrins, they're called.'

'Patrins? Yes, I've heard of those,' said Dick. 'Sticks and leaves arranged in certain patterns, or something, aren't they?'

'Yes,' said Henry. 'I know our gardener at home showed me an arrangement of sticks outside our back gate once, which he said was a message to any traveller following. He told me what it meant, too!'

'What did it mean?' asked Julian.

'It meant "Don't beg here. Mean people. No

good!"' said Henry, with a laugh. 'That's what he *said*, anyway!'

'We might ask the little traveller boy who came with the skewbald horse,' said Anne. 'He'll probably show us some messages. I'd like to learn some. You never know when anything like that could come in useful!'

'Yes. And we'll ask him why the travellers go to Mystery Moor,' said Julian, getting up and dusting the crumbs off his coat. 'They don't go there for nothing, you may be sure!'

'Where's old George gone?' asked Dick. 'I do hope she's not going to be silly.'

George was in one of the stables, grooming a horse so vigorously that it was most surprised. Swish-swish-swish-swish! What a brushing! George was working her intense annoyance out of herself. She mustn't spoil things for the boys and Anne! But oh, that horrible Henrietta, meeting them like that, pretending to be a boy. Heaving their luggage about, playing a joke on them! But surely they might have guessed!

'Oh, there you are, George,' said Dick's voice at the stable door. 'Let me help. Gosh, aren't you brown! Just as many freckles as ever!'

George grinned unwillingly. She tossed Dick the brush. 'Here you are, then! Do you and Ju want to go riding at all? There are plenty of horses to choose from here.'

Dick was relieved to see that George appeared to have got over her rage. 'Yes. It might be fun to go off for the day. What about tomorrow? We might explore a little of Mystery Moor.'

'Right,' said George. She began to heave some straw about. 'But not with That Girl,' she announced, from behind the straw she was carrying.

'What girl?' asked Dick, innocently. 'Oh, Henry, you mean? I keep thinking of her as a boy. No, we won't have her with us. We'll be just the five as usual.'

'That's all right then,' said George happily. 'Oh, here's Julian. Give a hand, Ju!'

It was lovely to have the two boys again, joking, laughing, teasing. They all went out in the fields that afternoon and heard the tales of the camp. It was just like old times, and Timmy was as pleased as anyone else. He went first to one of the four, then to another, licking each one as he went, his tail wagging vigorously.

'That's three times you've smacked me in the face with your tail, Timmy,' said Dick, dodging it. 'Can't you look behind yourself and see where my face is?'

'Woof,' said Timmy happily, and turned round to lick Dick, wagging his tail in Julian's face this time!

Somebody squeezed through the hedge behind them. George stiffened, feeling sure that it was Henrietta. Timmy barked sharply.

It wasn't Henrietta. It was the little traveller boy. He came up to them. There were tear streaks down his face.

'I've come for the horse,' he said. 'Do you know where he is?'

'He's not ready for walking yet,' said George. 'Captain Johnson told you he wouldn't be. What's the matter? Why have you been crying?'

'My father hit me,' said the boy. 'He cuffed me and knocked me right over.'

'Whatever for?' said Anne.

'Because I left the horse,' said the boy. 'My father said all it wanted was a bit of ointment and a bandage. He has to start off with the other caravans today, you see.'

'Well, you really *can't* have the horse yet,' said Anne. 'It isn't fit to walk, let alone drag a caravan. You don't want Captain Johnson to tell the police you're working it when it's not fit, do you? You know he means what he says?'

'Yes. But I must have the horse,' said the small boy. 'I daren't go back without it. My father would half kill me.'

'I suppose he doesn't care to come himself, so he sends you instead,' said Dick, in disgust.

The boy said nothing, and rubbed his sleeve across his face. He sniffed.

'Get your hanky,' said Dick.

'Please let me have my horse,' said the boy. 'I tell you, I'll be half killed if I go back without him.' He began to cry again.

The children felt sorry for him. He was such a thin, skinny misery of a boy, and goodness, how he sniffed all the time!

'What's your name?' asked Anne.

'Sniffer,' said the boy. 'That's what my father calls me.'

It was certainly a good name for him; but what a horrid father he must have!

'Haven't you got a proper name?' asked Anne.

'Yes. But I've forgotten it,' said Sniffer. 'Let me have my horse. I tell you, my father's waiting.'

Julian got up. 'I'll come and see your father and put some sense into him. Where is he?'

'Over there,' said Sniffer with a big sniff, and he pointed over the hedge. 'I'll come too,' said Dick. In the end everyone got up and went with Sniffer. They walked through the gate and saw a dark-faced, surly-looking man standing motionless not far off. His thick, oily hair was curly, and he wore enormous gold rings hanging from his ears. He looked up as the little company came near.

'Your horse isn't fit to walk yet,' said Julian.

'You can have it tomorrow or the next day, the captain says.'

'I'll have it now,' said the man, in a surly tone. 'We're starting off tonight or tomorrow over the moor. I can't wait.'

'But what's the hurry?' said Julian. 'The moor will wait for you!'

The man scowled and shifted from one foot to another. 'Can't you stay for another night or two and then go after the others?' said Dick.

'Listen, Father! You go with the other caravans,' said Sniffer, eagerly. 'Go in Moses' caravan and leave ours here. I can put our horse into the shafts tomorrow, or maybe the next day, and follow after!'

'But how would you know the way?' said George.

Sniffer made a scornful movement with his hand. 'Easy! They'll leave me patrins to follow,' he said.

'Oh yes,' said Dick, remembering. He turned to the silent traveller. 'Well, what about it? It seems that Sniffer here has quite a good idea, and you most certainly can't have the horse today anyway.'

The man turned and said something angry and scornful to poor Sniffer, who shrank away from the words as if they were blows. The four children couldn't understand a word, for it was all poured out in a language that they could not follow. Then the man turned on his heel and, without so much as a look at them, slouched away, his earrings gleaming as he went.

'What did he say?' asked Julian.

Sniffer gave one of his continual sniffs. 'He was very angry. He said he'd go with the others, and I could come on with Clip the horse, and drive our caravan,' he said. 'I'll be all right there tonight with Liz.'

'Who's Liz?' asked Anne, hoping that it was someone who would be kind to this poor little wretch.

'My dog,' said Sniffer, smiling for the first time. 'I left her behind because she sometimes goes for hens, and Captain Johnson doesn't like that.'

'I bet he doesn't,' said Julian. 'All right, that's settled then. You can come for Clip, or Clop, or whatever your horse is called, tomorrow, and we'll see if it's fit to walk.'

'I'm glad,' said Sniffer, rubbing his nose. 'I don't want Clip to go lame, see? But my father's very fierce.'

'So we gather,' said Julian, looking at a bruise on Sniffer's face. 'You come tomorrow and you can show us some of the patrins, the messages, that you use. We'd like to know some.'

'I'll come,' promised Sniffer, nodding his head vigorously. 'And you will come to see my caravan? I shall be all alone there, except for Liz.'

'Well, I suppose it would be something to do,' said Dick. 'Yes, we'll come. I hope it's not too smelly.'

'Smelly?' said Sniffer, surprised. 'I don't know. I will show you patrins there and Liz will show you her tricks. She is very, very clever. Once she belonged to a circus.'

'We must certainly take Timmy to see this clever dog,' said Anne, patting Timmy, who had been hunting for rabbits and had only just come back. 'Timmy, would you like to go and visit a very clever dog called Liz?'

'Woof,' said Timmy, wagging his tail politely.

'Right,' said Dick. 'I'm glad you approve, Tim. We'll all try and come tomorrow, Sniffer, after you've been to see how Clip is getting on. I don't somehow think you'll be able to have him then, though. We'll see!'

# [4]

# *A bed in the stable*

The boys slept in one of the stables that night.
Captain Johnson said they could either have
mattresses sent out, or could sleep in the straw,
with rugs.

'Oh, straw and rugs, please,' said Julian.
'That's fine. We'll be as snug as anything with
those.'

'I wish Anne and I could sleep in a stable too,'
said George, longingly. 'We never have. Can't
we, Captain Johnson?'

'No. You've got beds that you're paying for,'
said the captain. 'Anyway, girls can't do that
sort of thing, not even girls who try to be boys,
George!'

'I've *often* slept in a stable,' said Henrietta.
'At home when we've too many visitors, I always turn out and sleep in the straw.'

'Bad luck on the horses!' said George.

'Why?' demanded Henry at once.

'Because you must keep them awake all night with your snoring!' said George.

Henry snorted crossly and went out. It was maddening that she should snore at night, but she simply couldn't help it.

'Never mind!' George called after her. 'It's a nice *manly* snore, Henrietta!'

'Shut up, George,' said Dick, rather shocked at this sudden display of pettiness on George's part.

'Don't tell *me* to shut up,' said George. 'Tell Henrietta!'

'George, don't be an ass,' said Julian. But George didn't like that either, and stalked out of the room in just the same stiff, offended way that Henry had done!

'Oh dear!' said Anne. 'It's been like this all the time. First Henry, then George, then George, then Henry! They really are a couple of idiots!'

She went to see where the boys were to sleep.

They had been told to use a small stable, empty except for the traveller's horse that lay patiently down, its bandaged leg stretched out on the floor. Anne patted it and stroked it. It was an ugly little thing but its patient brown eyes were lovely.

The boys had heaps of straw to burrow into, and some old rugs. Anne thought it all looked lovely. 'You can wash and everything at the house,' she said. 'Then just slip over here to sleep. Doesn't it smell nice? All straw and hay and horse! I hope the horse won't disturb you. He may be a bit restless if his leg hurts him.'

'Nothing will disturb *us* tonight!' said Julian. 'What with camp life and open air and wind-on-the-hills and all that kind of thing, we're sure to sleep like logs. I think we're going to enjoy it here, Anne, very quiet and peaceful!'

George looked in at the door. 'I'll lend you Timmy if you like,' she said, anxious to make up for her display of temper.

'Oh, hallo, George! No thanks. I don't particularly want old Tim climbing over me all night long, trying to find the softest part of me to sleep on!' said Julian. 'I say, look, he's showing me how to make a good old burrow to sleep in! Hey, Tim, come out of my straw!'

Timmy had flung himself into the straw and was turning vigorously round and round in it as if he were making a bed for himself. He stood and looked up at them, his mouth open and his tongue hanging out at one side.

'He's laughing,' said Anne, and it did indeed look as if Timmy was having a good old laugh at them. Anne gave him a hug and he licked her lavishly, and then began to burrow round and round in the straw again.

Someone came up, whistling loudly, and put her head in at the door. 'I've brought you a couple of old pillows. Mrs Johnson said you'd better have something for your heads.'

'Oh thanks awfully, Henry,' said Julian, taking them.

'How kind of you, Henri*etta*,' said George.

'It's a pleasure, Geor*gina*,' said Henry, and the boys burst out laughing. Fortunately the supper-bell went just then and they all went across the yard at once. Somehow everyone was always hungry at the stables!

The girls looked very different in the evening, because they had to change out of their dirty, smelly jodhpurs or breeches and put on dresses. Anne, Henry and George hurried to change before Mrs Johnson rang the supper-bell again. She always gave them ten minutes' grace, knowing that they might sometimes have a job to finish with the horses, but everyone was supposed to be at the table when the second supper-bell had finished ringing.

George looked nice, because her curly hair went with a skirt and blouse quite well, but Henry looked quite wrong, somehow, in her frilly dress.

'You look like a boy dressed up!' said Anne, and this pleased Henry, but not George. The talk at the supper-table was mainly about all the wonderful things that Henry had done in her life. Apparently she had three brothers and did everything with them, and according to her own tales, she was considerably better than they were!

They had sailed a ship up to Norway. They had hiked from London to York.

'Was Dick Turpin with you?' inquired George, sarcastically. 'On his horse, Black Bess? I expect you got there long before *him*, didn't you?'

Henry took no notice. She went on with wonderful tales of her family's exploits, swimming across wide rivers, climbing Snowdon to the top, goodness, there wasn't a single thing she didn't seem to have done!

'You certainly ought to have been a boy, Henry,' said Mrs Johnson, which was exactly what Henry wanted everyone to say!

'Henry, when you've told us the story of how you climbed Mount Everest and got there before anyone else, perhaps you would finish your plateful,' said Captain Johnson, who got very tired of Henry's tongue.

George roared with laughter, not that she thought it was very funny, but because she loved any chance to laugh at Henry. Henry tackled the rest of her food at top speed. How she did love to hold everyone spellbound with her extraordinary tales! George didn't believe a word, but Dick and Julian thought it quite likely that this tall, wiry girl *could* do things just as well as her brothers.

There were a few jobs to be done after supper, and Henry kept well away from George, knowing quite well that she would have a few cutting things to say. Well, *she* didn't care! Everyone else thought she was marvellous! She tore off her frilly dress and put on jodhpurs again, although it would only be a short time before they all went to bed.

George and Anne went with the boys to their stable. They were in pyjamas and dressing-gowns, both yawning as they went. 'Got your torches?' said George. 'We're not allowed to have candles in the stables, because of the straw, you know. Good night! Sleep well! And I hope that that idiot of a Henry doesn't come along early in the morning, whistling like a paper-boy, and wake you up!'

'Nothing will wake me up tonight, nothing at all,' said Julian, with a huge yawn. He lay down in the straw and pulled an old rug over him. 'Oh, what a bed! Give me stable straw every time to sleep in!'

The girls laughed. The boys really *did* look very comfortable. 'Sleep tight,' said Anne, and walked off with George to the house.

Soon all the lights were out everywhere. Henry was asleep and snoring as usual. She had to have a separate room, otherwise she kept everyone awake! But even so, Anne and George could hear her, snoring away – rrrumph – rrrumph! rrrumph – RRRRUMPH!

'Blow Henrietta!' said George, sleepily. 'What a row she makes. Anne, she's not to come with us when we go riding tomorrow. Do you hear, Anne?'

'Not very well,' murmured Anne, trying to open her eyes. 'G'night, George!'

Timmy was on George's feet as usual. He lay snuggled there, eyes shut and ears asleep too. He got as tired as everyone else, running over the hills all day, scrabbling at scores of rabbit holes, chasing dozens of remarkably fleet-footed rabbits. But at night he too slept like a log.

Out in the stable the two boys slept peacefully, covered by the old rug. Nearby the little skewbald horse moved restlessly, but they heard nothing. An owl came swooping over the stable, looking for mice down below. It screeched loudly, hoping to scare a mouse into sudden flight. Then it would swoop down and take it into its talons.

Not even the screech awakened the boys. They slept dreamlessly, tired out.

The door of the stable was shut and latched. Clip, the horse, suddenly stirred and looked round at the door. The latch was moving! Someone was lifting it from the outside. Clip's pricked ears heard the sound of a little shuffle.

He watched the door. Who was coming? He hoped it was Sniffer, the boy he liked so much. Sniffer was always kind to him. He didn't like being away from Sniffer. He listened for the sniff-sniff that always went with the little boy, but he didn't hear it.

The door opened very slowly indeed. It gave no creak. Clip saw the night sky outside, set with stars. He made out a figure outlined against the darkness of the starry night, a black shadow.

Someone came into the stable, and whispered 'Clip!'

The horse gave a little whinny. It wasn't Sniffer's voice. It was his father's. Clip did not like him, he was too free with cuffs and kicks, and slashes with the whip. He lay still, wondering why the traveller had come.

The man had no idea that Dick and Julian were sleeping in the stable. He had come in quietly because he had thought there might be other horses there, and he did not want to startle them and make them stamp about in fright. He had no torch, but his keen eyes made out Clip at once, lying in his straw.

He tiptoed across to him and fell over Julian's feet, sticking out from the straw bed he was lying on. He fell with a thud, and Julian sat up very suddenly indeed, awake at once.

'Who's there! What is it?'

The traveller shrank down beside Clip, keeping silent. Julian began to wonder if he had been dreaming. But his foot distinctly hurt him. Surely somebody had trodden on it, or fallen over it? He woke Dick.

'Where's the torch? Hallo, look, the stable door is open! Quick, Dick, where on earth is the torch?'

They found it at last and Julian clicked it on. At first he saw nothing, for the man was in Clip's stall, lying down behind the horse. Then the torch picked him out.

'Hallo! Look there – it's that traveller, Sniffer's father!' said Julian. 'Get up, you! What on earth are you doing here, in the middle of the night?'

# [5]

## George gets a headache!

The man got up sullenly. His earrings shone in the light of the torch. 'I came to get Clip,' he said. 'He's my horse, isn't he?'

'You were told he wasn't fit to walk yet,' said Julian. 'Do you want him to go lame for life? You ought to know enough about horses to know when one can be worked or not!'

'I've got my orders,' said the man. 'I've got to take my caravan with the others.'

'Who said so?' said Dick, scornfully.

'Barney Boswell,' said the man. 'He's boss of our lot here. We've got to start off together tomorrow.'

'But why?' said Julian, puzzled. 'What's so urgent about all this? What's the mystery?'

'There isn't any mystery,' said the man, still sullen. 'We're just going to the moor.'

'What are you going to do there?' asked Dick, curiously. 'It doesn't seem to me to be the place to take a lot of caravans to. There's nothing there at all, is there? Or so I've heard.'

The man shrugged his shoulders and said nothing. He turned to Clip as if to get him up. But Julian rapped out at him at once.

'Oh no, you don't! If you don't care about injuring a horse, I do! You've only got to be patient for a day or two more, and he'll be quite all right. You're not to take him tonight. Dick, go and wake Captain Johnson. He'll know what to do.'

'No,' said the man, scowling. 'Don't wake anybody. I'll go. But just see that Clip is given to Sniffer as soon as it's possible, or I'll know the reason why! See?'

He looked at Julian in a threatening way.

'Take that scowl off your face,' said Julian. 'I'm glad you've seen sense. Clear out now. Go off with the others tomorrow and I'll see that Sniffer has the horse in a short time.'

The man moved to the door and slid out like

a shadow. Julian went to watch him across the yard, wondering whether, out of spite, the man might try to steal a hen, or one of the ducks sleeping beside the pond.

But there was no sudden clucking, no loud quack. The man had gone as silently as he had come.

'Most peculiar, all this!' said Julian, latching the door again. He tied a piece of thick string over it his side, so that it could not be lifted from outside. 'There! Now if the traveller comes again, he'll find he can't get in. What a nerve, coming here in the middle of the night like that!'

He got back into the straw. 'He must have fallen right over my foot,' he said, snuggling down. 'He woke me up with an awful jump. Good thing for Clip that we were sleeping out here tonight, or he'd be dragging along a heavy caravan tomorrow, and going lame again. I don't like that fellow!'

He fell asleep again and so did Dick. Clip slept too, his leg feeling easier. How glad he had been that day not to have to drag along the heavy caravan!

The boys told Captain Johnson next morning about the traveller's midnight visit. He nodded. 'Yes, I ought to have warned you that he might come. They're not always very good to their horses. Well, I'm glad you sent him off. I don't reckon Clip's leg will be ready for walking on till the day after tomorrow. There's no harm in giving the poor creature a few days' rest. Sniffer can easily take the caravan on after the others.'

It looked as if that day was going to be fun. After all the horses had been seen to, and many odd jobs done, the four, with Timmy, planned to set out for a day's ride. Captain Johnson said he would let Julian ride his own sturdy cob and Dick took a bonny chestnut horse with four white socks. The girls had the horses they usually rode.

Henry hung about, looking very mournful. The boys felt quite uncomfortable. 'We *really* ought to tell her to come along too,' said Dick to Julian. 'It seems jolly mean to leave her behind with those little kids.'

'Yes, I know. I agree with you,' said Julian. 'Anne, come here! Can't you suggest to George that we take Henry too? She's longing to come, I know.'

'Yes, she is,' said Anne. 'I feel awful about it. But George will be mad if we ask Henry. They really do get on each other's nerves. I simply daren't ask George to let Henry come, Ju.'

'But this is *silly*!' said Julian. 'To think we don't *dare* to ask George to let somebody come! George will have to learn sense. I like Henry. She's boastful, and I don't believe half the tales she tells, but she's a sport and good fun. Hey, Henry!'

'Coming!' yelled Henry, and came running, looking very hopeful.

'Would you like to come with us!' said Julian. 'We're all going off for the day. Have you got any jobs to do, or can you come?'

'Can I *come*! You bet!' said Henry, joyfully. 'But – does George know?'

'I'll soon tell her,' said Julian, and went in search of George. She was helping Mrs Johnson to get saddle-bags ready, full of food.

'George,' said Julian, boldly, 'Henry is coming too. Will there be enough food for everyone?'

'Oh! How *nice* of you to ask her!' said Mrs Johnson, sounding very pleased. 'She's dying to come. She's been so good this week, too, while we've been short-handed. She deserves a treat. Isn't that *nice*, George?'

George muttered something peculiar and went out of the room, her face scarlet. Julian stared after her, his eyebrows cocked in a comical manner.

'I don't somehow feel that George thinks it's nice,' he said. 'I feel as if we are in for an awkward day, Mrs Johnson.'

'Oh, don't take any notice of George when she's silly,' said Mrs Johnson, comfortably, filling another paper bag with delicious-looking sandwiches. 'And don't take any notice of Henry, either, when she's idiotic. There! If you get through all this food, I shall be surprised!'

William, one of the younger ones, came in just then. 'What a lot of food you've given them,' he said. 'Will there be enough left for *us* to have today?'

'Good gracious, yes!' said Mrs Johnson. 'You think of nothing but your tummy, William! Go and find George and tell her the food is ready for her to put into the saddle-bags.'

William disappeared and then came back. 'George says she's got a headache and doesn't think she'll go on the ride,' he announced.

Julian looked startled and upset. 'Now listen to me, Julian,' said Mrs Johnson, beginning to insert the parcels of food carefully into the saddle-bags, 'just leave her to her imaginary headache. Don't go fussing round her, and begging her to come and saying you won't have Henry. Just believe quite firmly in her headache, and go off by yourselves. It's the quickest way to make George see sense, believe *me*!'

'Yes, I think you're right,' said Julian, frowning. To think that George should behave like a sulky little girl, after all the adventures they had been through together! Just because of Henry. It really was absurd.

'Where *is* George?' he said to William.

'Up in her room,' said William, who had been engrossed in picking up and eating all the crumbs he could. Julian went out of the room and into the yard. He knew which window belonged to the room where George and Anne slept. He yelled up.

'George! Sorry about your headache! Sure you don't feel like coming?'

'No!' came back an answering shout, and the window was shut down with a slam.

'OK! Awfully disappointed and all that!' shouted Julian. 'Do hope your head will soon be better! See you later!'

No other reply came from the window, but, as Julian went across the yard to the stables, a very surprised face watched him go, from behind the bedroom curtains. George was extremely astonished to have been taken at her word, shocked at being left behind after all, and angry with Henry and everyone else for putting her into this fix!

Julian told the others that George had a

headache and wasn't coming. Anne was most concerned and wanted to go and comfort her but Julian forbade her to.

'No. She's up in her room. Leave her alone, Anne. That's an order – OK?'

'All right,' said Anne, half-relieved. She felt sure that George's headache was mostly temper, and she didn't at all want to go and argue with her for half an hour. Henry hadn't said a word. She had flushed with surprise when Julian had announced that George was not coming, and she knew at once that there was no real headache! *She* was George's headache, she knew that!

She went up to Julian. 'Look, I guess it's because you've asked *me* to come, that Georgina won't come with us. I don't want to spoil things. You go and tell her I'm not going after all.'

Julian looked at Henry gratefully. 'That's jolly nice of you,' he said. 'But we're taking George at her word. Anyway, we didn't ask you out of politeness. We *wanted* you to come!'

'Thanks,' said Henry. 'Well, let's go before anything else happens! Our horses are ready. I'll fix the saddle-bags.'

Soon all four were on their horses, and were walking over the yard to the gate. George heard the clippity-clop-clippity-clop of the hooves and peeped out of the window again. They were going after all! She hadn't thought they really *would* go without her. She was horrified.

Why did I behave like that? I've put myself in the wrong! thought poor George. Now Henrietta will be with them all day and will be as nice as possible, just to show me up. What an ass I am! 'Timmy, I'm an ass and an idiot, and a great big idiot! Aren't I?'

Timmy didn't think so. He had been puzzled to hear the others going off without him and George, and had gone to the door and whined. Now he came back to George and put his head on her knee. He knew George was not happy.

'*You* don't care how I behave, do you, Tim?' said George, stroking the soft, furry head. 'That's the best thing about a dog! You don't care if I'm in the wrong or not, you just love me all the same, don't you? Well, you shouldn't love me today, Tim. I've been an idiot!'

There was a knock at her door. It was William again. 'George! Mrs Johnson says, if your headache is bad, undress and get into bed. But if it's better, come down and help with Clip, the traveller's horse.'

'I'll come down,' said George, flinging away her sulks at one go. 'Tell Mrs Johnson I'll go to the stable at once.'

'All right,' said the stolid William, and trotted off like a reliable little pony.

George went downstairs with Timmy, and into the yard. She wondered how far the others had gone. She couldn't see them in the distance. Would they have a good day together, with that horrid Henry? Ugh!

The others were almost a mile away, cantering easily. What *fun*! A whole day before them, on Mystery Moor!

# [6]

## A grand day

'I think it's a jolly good name, Mystery Moor,' said Dick, as the four of them went along. 'Look at it stretching for miles, all blazing with gorse.'

'I don't think it looks at all mysterious,' said Henry, surprised.

'Well, it's got a sort of quietness and broodiness,' said Anne, 'as if something big happened long ago in the past and it's waiting for something to happen again.'

'Quiet and broody? It sounds like one of the farmyard hens sitting on her eggs!' said Henry with a laugh. 'I think it might be a bit frightening and mysterious at night, but it's just an ordinary stretch of country in the daytime, fine for riding over. I can't think why it's called Mystery Moor.'

'We'll have to look it up in some book that tells about this part of the country,' said Dick. 'I expect it was called that because of some strange happening or other, hundreds of years ago, when people believed in witches and things like that.'

They followed no road or path, but rode where they pleased. There were great stretches of wiry grass, masses of heather springing up afresh, and, blazing its gold everywhere on this lovely April day, was the gorse.

Anne sniffed continually as they rode past the gorse bushes. Dick looked at her.

'You sound like Sniffer!' he said. 'Have you got a cold?'

Anne laughed. 'No, of course not. But I do so love the smell of the gorse. What does it smell of? Vanilla? Hot coconut? It's a lovely *warm* smell!'

'Look! What's that moving over there?' said Julian, suddenly reining in his horse. They all strained their eyes to see.

'It's caravans!' said Julian, at last. 'Of course! They were setting out today, weren't they?

Well, they must find it very rough going, that's all I can say. There's no real road anywhere, as far as I can see.'

'Where can they be going?' wondered Anne. 'What's over in that direction?'

'They'll come to the coast if they keep on the way they are going,' said Julian, considering. 'Let's ride over and have a look at them, shall we?'

'Yes. Good idea!' said Dick. So they turned their horses' heads to the right, and rode towards the faraway caravans. These made quite a splash of colour as they went along. There were four of them – two red ones, a blue one and a yellow one. They went very slowly indeed, each pulled by a small, wiry horse.

'They all look like skewbalds, brown and white,' said Dick. 'It's funny that so many travellers have skewbald horses. I wonder why it is?'

They heard shouting as they came near the caravans, and saw one man pointing them out to another. It was Sniffer's father!

'Look, that's the fellow who woke us up in the stable last night,' said Julian to Dick. 'Sniffer's father! What a nasty bit of work he is! Why doesn't he get a hair cut?'

'Good morning!' called Dick, as they rode up to the caravans on their horses. 'Nice day!'

There was no answer. The travellers driving their caravans, and those walking alongside, looked sourly at the four riders.

'Where are you going?' asked Henry. 'To the coast?'

'It's nothing to do with you,' said one of the travellers, an old man with curly grey hair.

'Surly folk, aren't they?' said Dick to Julian. 'I suppose they think we're spying on them, or something. I wonder how they manage about food on this moor, no shops or anything. I suppose they take it all with them.'

'I'll ask them,' said Henry, not at all put off by the surly looks. She rode right up to Sniffer's father.

'How do you manage about food and water?' she asked.

'We've got food there,' said Sniffer's father, jerking his head back towards one of the caravans. 'As for water, we know where the springs are.'

'Are you camping on the moor for a long time?' asked Henry, thinking that a traveller's life might be a fine one, for a time! Fancy living out here on this lovely moor with gorse blazing gold all around, and primroses by the thousand in the sheltered corners!

'That's nothing to do with *you*!' shouted the old man with curly grey hair. 'Clear off and leave us alone!'

'Come on, Henry,' said Julian, swinging round to go off. 'They don't like us asking them questions. They think it's prying, not interest. Maybe they have lots of things to hide, and don't want us poking around – one or two chickens from a farm, a duck or so from the pond. They live from hand to mouth, these folk.'

Some bright-eyed children peered from the vans as they went by. One or two were running outside, but they sheered off like frightened rabbits when Henry cantered towards them.

'Oh well, they simply don't *want* to be friendly,' she said, and went to join the other three. 'What a strange life they lead, in their houses on wheels! Never staying anywhere for long, always on the move. Get up, there, Sultan. Go after the others!'

Her horse obediently followed the other three, taking care not to step into any rabbit holes! What fun it was to be out here in the sunshine, jogging up and down on the horse's back, without a care in the world! Henry was very happy.

The other three were enjoying their day, but they were not quite so happy. They kept wondering about George. They missed Timmy too. He should be trotting beside them, enjoying the day as well!

They lost sight of the caravans after a time. Julian kept track of the way they went, half-afraid of being lost. He had a compass with him, and checked their direction continually. 'It would never do to have to spend a night out here!' he said. 'Nobody would ever find us!'

They had a magnificent lunch about half past twelve. Really, Mrs Johnson had surpassed herself! Egg and sardine sandwiches, tomato and lettuce, ham – there seemed no end to them! Great slices of cherry cake were added too, and a large, juicy pear each.

'I like this kind of cherry cake,' said Dick, looking at his enormous slice. 'The cherries have all gone to the bottom. They make a very nice last mouthful!'

'Any drinks?' said Henry, and was handed a bottle of ginger-beer. She drank it thirstily.

'Why does ginger-beer taste so nice on a picnic?' she said. '*Much* nicer than drinking it sitting down in a shop, even if it's got ice in it!'

'There's a spring or something nearby,' said Julian. 'I can hear it bubbling.'

They all listened. Yes, there was a little bubbling, tinkling noise. Anne got up to trace it. She found it in a few minutes and called the others. There was a round pool, cool and blue, lying two or three feet down, and into it, from one side, fell a crystal-clear spring of water, tinkling as it fell.

'One of the springs that the travellers use, when they come to this deserted moor, I expect,' said Julian. He cupped his hands under the falling water and got his palms full. He carried the water to his mouth and sipped it.

'Delicious! Cool as an ice-box,' he said. 'Taste it, Anne.'

They rode a little farther, but the moor seemed the same everywhere, heather, wiry grass, gorse, a clear spring falling into a pool or tiny stream here and there, and a few trees, mostly silver birch.

Larks sang all the time, soaring high in the air, almost too far up to see.

'Their song falls down like raindrops,' said Anne, holding out her hands as if to catch them. Henry laughed. She liked this family, and was very glad they had asked her to come out with them. She thought George was silly to have stayed at the stables.

'I think we ought to get home,' said Julian at last, looking at his watch. 'We're a good way away. Let me see now. We want to make more or less for the setting sun. Come on!'

He led the way, his horse picking its own path over the heather. The others followed. Dick stopped after a while.

'Are you sure we're quite right, Ju? I don't somehow feel that we are. The moor is different here, rather sandy and not so much gorse.'

Julian stopped his horse and looked round and about. 'Yes, it does look a bit different,' he said. 'But yet we seem to be going in the right direction. Let's go a bit more to the west. If only there was something on the horizon to guide us. But this moor hasn't a thing that stands out anywhere!'

They went on again, and then Henry gave an exclamation. 'I say! What's this? Do come here.'

The two boys and Anne swerved over to Henry. She was now off her horse, and was bending over, scraping away at the heather.

'Look, it seems like rails, or something,' said Henry. 'Very old and rusty. But they can't be surely?'

Everyone was now down on their knees, scraping sand and heather away. Julian sat back and considered.

'Yes, it's rails. Old ones, as you say. But what in the world were rails laid down here for?'

'I can't think,' said Henry. 'I only caught sight of them by chance, they're so overgrown. I couldn't believe my eyes!'

'They must lead from somewhere *to* somewhere!' said Dick. 'Perhaps there was a quarry or something on the moor and they ran little engines with trucks there, to fetch the sand, and take it back to town to sell.'

'That's about it,' said Julian. 'It's very sandy here, as we noticed. Good, fine sand. Maybe there is a quarry on the moor. Well, *that* way, behind us, goes right out on the moor, so *this* way must lead back to some town or village, probably Milling Green or somewhere like that.'

'Yes. You're right,' said Dick. 'In which case, if we follow the lines along, we'll get back to civilisation sooner or later!'

'Well, seeing that we seem to be more or less lost, that would be quite a good idea!' said Henry. She mounted her horse again and rode along the lines.

'They're fairly easy to see!' she called. 'If you ride between them, that is, because they go so straight.'

The lines ran steadily over the moor, sometimes very overgrown, and in about half an hour's time Henry gave a cry and pointed forward. 'Houses! I thought we'd soon come to some place!'

'It *is* Milling Green!' said Julian, as the rails came to a sudden end, and they rode out into a small cart road.

'Well, we haven't far to go now, to get to the stables,' said Henry, pleased. 'I say, wouldn't it be fun to follow those lines all across the moor and see where they really lead to?'

'Yes. We might do that one day,' said Julian.

'Gosh, it's getting late. I wonder how old George has been getting on today!'

They walked quickly along to the stables, thinking of George. Would she have retired to bed? Would she still be cross, or worse still, hurt and grieved? It was anybody's guess!

# George, Sniffer and Liz

George had had quite an interesting day. First she had gone down to help Captain Johnson do Clip's leg again and bandage it up. The little skewbald stood very patiently, and George felt a sudden liking for the ugly little creature.

'Thanks, George,' said Captain Johnson, who, to her relief, had said nothing about her not having gone riding with the others. 'Now would you like to come and put jumps up for the youngsters? They're longing to do some more jumping.'

George found that it was quite amusing to teach the younger ones how to jump. They were so very, very proud of themselves when they went over even a foot-high jump on their little ponies.

After that Sniffer arrived, accompanied by a

peculiar little mongrel called Liz. Liz was a bit of a spaniel, a bit of a poodle, and odd bits of something else – and looked rather like a small, walking hearth-rug of black curly fur.

Timmy was amazed to see this walking mat, and sat and watched Liz sniffing here and there for some time, before he came to the conclusion that it really *was* some kind of dog. He gave a sharp little bark to see what this comical creature would do when she heard it.

Liz took no notice at all. She had unearthed a small bone, which smelt extremely interesting. Timmy considered that all bones within the radius of at least a mile belonged to him and him alone. So he ran over to Liz at once and gave a small, warning growl.

Liz immediately dropped the bone humbly at his feet, then sat up on her hind-legs and begged. Timmy eyed her in astonishment. Then Liz stood up on her hind-legs and walked daintily all round Timmy and back again.

Timmy was astounded. He had never seen a

dog do that before. *Could* this hearth-rug affair be a dog after all?

Liz saw that Timmy was really impressed, and went on with yet another trick she had learnt during the time she had been with the circus.

She turned head-over-heels, yapping all the time. Timmy retreated a few steps into the bushes. This was going *too* far! What was this animal doing? Trying to stand on its head?

Liz went on turning head-over-heels very rapidly and ended up almost on Timmy's front paws. He had now backed into the bush as far as he could.

Liz remained on her back, paws in the air, tongue hanging out, panting. She gave a very small, beseeching whine.

Timmy bent his head down and sniffed at her paws. Behind him his tail began to move a little, yes, it had a wag in it! He sniffed again. Liz leapt on to her four feet and pranced all round Timmy, yapping as if to say 'Come on and play! Do come!'

And then suddenly Timmy fell upon the absurd little creature and pretended to worry it. Liz gave a delighted volley of yaps and rolled over and over. They had a marvellous game, and when it was all over, Timmy sank down, panting for breath, in a sunny corner of the yard and Liz settled herself between his front paws, as if she had known him all her life!

When George came out of the stable with Sniffer, she could hardly believe her eyes. 'What's that Timmy's got between his paws?' she said. 'It's surely not a *dog*!'

'It's Liz,' said Sniffer. 'She can get round any dog there is, George! Liz! You're a monkey, aren't you! Walk, then, walk!'

Liz left Timmy and ran over to Sniffer, walking daintily on her hind legs. George laughed. 'What a funny little creature, like a bit cut out of a furry hearth-rug!'

'She's clever,' said Sniffer and patted Liz. 'Well, George, when can I have Clip, do you think? My father has gone off with the other caravans and he's left me with ours. So it doesn't matter whether it's today or tomorrow, or even the next day.'

'Well, it won't be today, that's certain,' said George. 'It might perhaps be tomorrow. Haven't you got a hanky, Sniffer? I never in my life heard anyone sniff as often as you do!'

Sniffer rubbed his sleeve across his nose. 'I've never had a hanky,' he said. 'But I've got my sleeve!'

'I think you're quite disgusting,' said George. 'I'm going to give you one of my own hankies, and you're to use it. You're *not* to keep sniffing like that.'

'Didn't know I did,' said Sniffer, half sulkily. 'What does it matter, anyway?'

But George had gone indoors and up the stairs. She chose a large hanky, in red and white stripes. That would do nicely for Sniffer! She took it down to him. He looked at it in surprise.

'That's a scarf for my neck!' he said.

'No, it isn't. It's a hanky for your nose,' said George. 'Haven't you a pocket to put it in?

That's right. Now, use it instead of sniffing, for goodness' sake!'

'Where are the others?' asked Sniffer, putting the hanky carefully into his pocket, almost as if it were made of glass.

'Gone riding,' said George, shortly.

'They said they would come and see my caravan,' said Sniffer. 'They said so!'

'Well, they won't be able to today,' said George. 'They'll be back too late, I expect. I'll come and see it, though. There's nobody in it, is there?'

George was not keen on meeting Sniffer's father or any other of his relations! He shook his head. 'No, it's empty. My father's gone, I told you, and my aunt and my grandma too.'

'What do you *do* on the moor?' asked George, as she followed Sniffer across the field and up the hill to where the caravans had stood. Now only one was left – Sniffer's.

'Play around,' said Sniffer, and gave an enormous sniff. George gave him a shove in the back.

'Sniffer! What did I give you the hanky for? *Don't* do that! It gets on my nerves!'

Sniffer used his sleeve at once, but fortunately George didn't notice. She had now come to the caravan and was staring at it. She thought of Sniffer's answer to her question a minute or two back.

'You said you just played around on the moor. But what does your *father* do, and your uncle and grandad and all the rest of the men? There's nothing to do there at all, as far as I can see, and no farmhouse to beg eggs or milk or anything from.'

Sniffer shut up like a clam. He was just about to sniff and thought better of it. He stared at George, his mouth set in an obstinate line.

George looked at him impatiently. 'Captain Johnson said you and your caravans went there every three months,' she said. 'What for? There must be *some* reason?'

'Well,' said Sniffer, looking away from her, 'we make pegs, and baskets, and—'

'I know that! All travellers make things to

sell,' said George. 'But you don't need to go into the middle of a deserted moor to make them. You can do them just as well in a village, or sitting in a field near a farmhouse. *Why* go to such a lonely place as the moor?'

Sniffer said nothing, but bent over an odd little arrangement of sticks set on the path beside his caravan. George saw them and bent over them too, her question forgotten.

'Oh! Is that a patrin? A traveller message! What does it mean?'

There were two sticks, one long and one short, neatly arranged in the shape of a cross. A little farther up on the path were a few single, straight sticks, all pointing in the same direction.

'Yes,' said Sniffer, very glad to have the subject changed. 'It's our way of telling things to those who may come after us. See the sticks in the shape of the cross? That's a patrin that says we've been along this way and we're going in the direction that the long stick points.'

'I see,' said George. 'How simple! But what

about these four straight sticks, all pointing the same way too. What do *they* mean?'

'They mean that the travellers went in caravans,' said Sniffer, giving a sudden sniff. 'See, four sticks, four caravans, going that way!'

'I *see*,' said George, making up her mind that she herself would evolve quite a few 'patrins' for use at school when they went for walks. 'Are there any more "patrins", Sniffer?'

'Plenty,' said the boy. 'Look, when I leave here, I shall put a patrin like this!' He picked a large leaf from a nearby tree, and then a small one. He placed them side by side, and weighted them down with small stones.

'What in the world does that mean?' said George.

'Well, it's a patrin, a message, to say that me and my little dog have gone in the caravan too,' said Sniffer, picking up the leaves. 'Suppose my father came back to find me, and he saw those leaves there, he'd know I'd gone on with my dog. It's simple. Big leaf for me, little leaf for my dog!'

'Yes. I like it,' said George, pleased. 'Now let's look at the caravan.'

It was an old-fashioned kind of caravan, not very big, and with huge wheels. The door and the steps down were in front. The shafts rested on the ground waiting for Clip to come back. The caravan was black with red designs on it here and there.

George went up the steps. 'I've been inside a few caravans,' she said. 'But never one quite like this.'

She peeped in curiously. It certainly wasn't very clean, but it wasn't as dirty as she expected either.

'It's not smelly, is it?' said Sniffer, quite anxiously. 'I tidied it up today, seeing as how I thought you were all visiting me. That's our bed at the back. We all sleep on it.'

George stared at the big bunk-like bed stretched at the end of the caravan, covered with a bright quilt. She imagined the whole family sleeping there, close together. Well, at least they would be warm in the winter.

'Don't you get hot in the summer, sleeping in this small caravan?' asked George.

'Oh no, only my grandma sleeps here then,' said Sniffer, swallowing a sniff in a hurry, before George could hear it. 'Me and the others sleep under the caravan. Then if it rains it doesn't matter.'

'Well, thanks for showing me so many things,' said George, looking round at the cupboards, the little locker-seats, and the over-big chest of drawers. 'How you all get in here is a miracle.'

She didn't go in. Even though Sniffer had tidied up, there was still a distinctly peculiar smell hanging about!

'Come and see us tomorrow, Sniffer,' she said, going down the steps. 'Clip may be all right by then. And Sniffer, don't you forget you've got a hanky now.'

'I won't forget,' said Sniffer proudly. 'I'll keep it as clean as can be, George!'

# [8]

## Sniffer makes a promise

George was feeling very lonely by the time the evening came. How had the others got on without her? Had they missed her at all? Perhaps they hadn't even *thought* of her!

'Anyway, they didn't have *you*, Timmy!' said George. 'You wouldn't go off and leave me, would you?'

Timmy pressed against her, glad to see that she was happier again. He wondered where the others were, and where they had gone to all day.

There was suddenly a clattering of hooves in the stable-yard and George flew to the door. Yes, they were back! How should she behave? She felt cross and relieved and rather humble and glad all at once! She stood there, not knowing whether to frown or to smile.

The others made up her mind for her. 'Hallo, George!' shouted Dick. 'We did miss you!'

'How's your head?' called Anne. 'I hope it's better!'

'Hallo!' called Henry. 'You ought to have come. We've had a super day!'

'Come and help us stable the horses, George,' shouted Julian. 'Tell us what you've been doing!'

Timmy had sped over to them, barking in delight. George found her legs running towards them too, a welcoming smile on her face.

'Hallo!' she called. 'Let me help! Did you really miss me? I missed you too.'

The boys were very relieved to see that George was herself again. Nothing more was said about her headache! She busied herself unsaddling the horses and listening to their story of the day. Then she told them about Sniffer and his patrins, and how she had given him a brand-new handkerchief.

'But I'm sure he thinks he's got to keep it spotlessly clean!' she said. 'He never used it

once when I was with him. There's the supper-
bell, we'll only *just* be in time! Are you hungry?'

'You bet we are!' said Dick. 'Though after
Mrs Johnson's sandwiches I never thought
I'd be able to eat any supper at all. How's
Clip?'

'Never mind now. I'll tell you everything at
supper,' said George. 'Do you want any help,
Henry?'

Henry was surprised to hear George call her
Henry instead of Henrietta. 'No thanks – er –
George,' she said. 'I can manage.'

It was a very jolly supper-time that evening.
The youngsters were set at a table by themselves, so the older ones talked to their heart's
content.

Captain Johnson was very interested to hear
about the old railway they had found. 'I never
knew there was anything like that on the
moors,' he said. 'Though of course, we've only
been here about fifteen years, so we don't know
a great deal of the local history. You want to go
and ask old Ben the blacksmith about that. He's

lived here all his life, and a long life it is, for he's over eighty!'

'Well, we've got to take some of the horses to be shod tomorrow, haven't we?' said Henry, eagerly. 'We could ask him then! Why, he might even have helped to make the rails!'

'We saw the caravans, George, when we had got pretty far out on the moor,' said Julian. 'Goodness knows where they were heading for, towards the coast, I should think. What's the coast like beyond the moor, Captain Johnson?'

'Wild,' said the captain. 'Great, unclimbable cliffs, and reefs or rocks stretching out to sea. Only the birds live there. There's no swimming, no boating, no beach.'

'Well, it beats me where those caravans are going,' said Dick. 'It's a mystery. They go every three months, don't they?'

'About that,' said Captain Johnson. 'I've no idea what the attraction of the moor is for the travellers. It just beats me! Usually they won't go anywhere there aren't a few farms, or at least a small village where they can sell their goods.'

'I'd like to go after them and see where they are and what they're doing,' said Julian, eating his third hard-boiled egg.

'All right. Let's,' said George.

'But how? We don't know where they've gone,' said Henry.

'Well, Sniffer's going to join them tomorrow, or as soon as Clip is all right for walking,' said George. 'And he's got to follow the patrins left on the way by the others. He says that he looks at the places where fires have been made on the way, and beside them somewhere he will see the patrins, the sticks that point in the direction he must follow.'

'He's sure to destroy them,' said Dick. 'We couldn't follow them!'

'We'll ask him to leave his *own* patrins,' said George. 'I think he will. He's not a bad little boy, really. I could ask him to leave *plenty* of patrins, so that we could easily find the way.'

'Well, it might be fun to see if we could read the right road to go, just as easily as the travellers do,' said Julian. 'We could make it a day's ride. It would be interesting!'

Henry gave a most enormous yawn, and that made Anne yawn too, though hers was a very polite one.

'Henry!' said Mrs Johnson.

'Sorry,' said Henry. 'It just came almost like a sneeze does. I don't know why, but I feel almost asleep.'

'Go to bed then,' said Mrs Johnson. 'You've had such a day of air and sunshine! You all look very brown too. The April sun has been as hot as July today.'

The five of them, and Timmy, went out for a last look at the horses, and to do one or two small jobs. Henry yawned again, and that set everyone else off, even George.

'Me for the straw!' said Julian, with a laugh. 'Oh, the thought of that warm, comfy straw bed is too good for words! You girls are welcome to the beds!'

'I hope Sniffer's pa doesn't come in the middle of the night again,' said Dick.

'I shall tie up the latch,' said Julian. 'Well, let's go and say good night to Mrs Johnson.'

It wasn't long before the three girls were in bed and the two boys cuddled down in the straw of the stable. Clip was there still, but he no longer fidgeted. He lay down quietly, and did not once move his bad leg. It was getting much better. He would certainly be able to go after the others the next day!

Julian and Dick fell asleep at once. No one came creeping in at the stable door that night. Nothing disturbed them until the morning, when a cock got into the stable through a window, sat on a rafter just above them, and crowed loudly enough to wake both boys with a jump.

'What's that!' said Dick. 'That awful screeching in my ear! Was it you, Ju?'

The cock crowed again and the boys laughed. 'Blow him!' said Julian, settling down again. 'I could do with another couple of hours' sleep!'

That morning Sniffer came slipping in at the

gate again. He never came boldly in; he slid through the hedge, or crept in at the gate, or appeared round a corner. He saw George and went over to her.

'George,' he called. 'Is Clip better?'

'Yes!' called back George. 'Captain Johnson says you can take him today. But wait a bit, Sniffer, I want to ask you something before you go.'

Sniffer was pleased. He liked this girl who had presented him with such a magnificent handkerchief. He took it carefully out of his pocket, hoping to please her.

'See,' he said. 'How clean it is! I have kept it very carefully.' He sniffed loudly.

'You're an idiot,' said George, exasperated. 'I gave it to you to *use*, not to keep clean in your pocket. It's to stop your *sniffing*. Honestly, you're a bit of a mutt, Sniffer. I shall take that hanky away if you don't use it!'

Sniffer looked alarmed. He shook it out carefully and then lightly touched his nose with it. He then folded it up conscientiously in the right creases and put it back into his pocket again.

'Now, NO sniffing!' commanded George, trying not to laugh. 'Listen, Sniffer, you know those patrins you showed me yesterday?'

'Yes, George,' said Sniffer.

'Well, will the other travellers who have gone in front, leave you patrins to follow, so that you will know the way?' said George.

Sniffer nodded. 'Yes, but not many, because I have been that way twice before. They will only leave them in places where I might go wrong.'

'I see,' said George. 'Now Sniffer, we want to have a sort of game. We want to see which of us can follow patrins, and we want you to lay patrins for us quite often, on your way to your family today. Will you?'

'Oh yes, I will,' said Sniffer, quite proud to have a favour asked of him. 'I will lay the ones I showed you, the cross, the long sticks, and the big and little leaf.'

'Yes, do,' said George. 'That will mean that

you have passed in a certain direction and you are a boy and a dog. That's right, isn't it?'

· 'Yes,' said Sniffer, nodding his head. 'You have remembered!'

'Right. And we're going to have a kind of game, trying to pretend we are travellers following others who have passed,' said George.

'You must not show yourselves when you come up to our caravans,' said Sniffer, looking suddenly alarmed. 'I should get into trouble for laying patrins for you.'

'All right. We'll be careful,' said George. 'Now let's go and get Clip.'

They fetched the patient little skewbald who came out gladly. He no longer limped, and his rest seemed to have done him good. He went off at a good pace with Sniffer. The last George heard of them was a very loud sniff indeed!

'Sniffer!' she shouted, warningly. He put his hand in his pocket and pulled out the hanky. He waved it gaily in the air, a sudden grin lighting up his face.

George went to find the others. 'Sniffer has

taken Clip,' she said. 'What about going down to the blacksmith, and taking those horses that want shoeing?'

'Good idea,' said Julian. 'We can ask him all about Mystery Moor then, and the strange little railway line, or whatever it is! Come on.'

They took the horses that needed shoeing. There were six of them, so they each rode one, and Julian led the sixth. Timmy ran happily along beside them. He loved the horses, and they regarded him as a real friend, bending their long noses down to sniff at him, whenever he came near.

They went slowly down the long lane to the blacksmith's. 'There it is!' said George. 'A proper old smithy with a lovely fire! And there's the smith!'

Old Ben was a mighty figure of a man, even though he was over eighty. He didn't shoe many horses now, but sat in the sun, watching all that was going on. He had a great mane of white hair, and eyes that were as black as the coal he had so many times heated to a fiery flame.

'Good morning, young masters and Miss,' he said and Julian grinned. That would please George and Henry!

'We've got some questions to ask you,' said George dismounting.

'Ask away!' said the old man. 'If it's about this place, there's nothing much old Ben can't tell you! Give Jim your horses. Now, ask away!'

# *The blacksmith tells a tale*

'Well,' began Julian, 'we went riding on Mystery Moor yesterday, and for one thing we'd like to know if there is any reason for the curious name. *Was* there ever a mystery on that moor?'

'Oh, there were plenty of mysteries away there,' said Old Ben. 'People lost and never come back again, noises that no one could find the reason of . . .'

'What kind of noises?' said Anne, curiously.

'Ah now, when I was a boy, I spent nights up on that moor,' said old Ben, solemnly, 'and the noises that went on there! Screeches and howls and the like, and moans and the sweep of big wings . . .'

'Well, all that might have been owls and foxes and things like that,' said Dick. 'I've heard a barn owl give a screech just over my head which made me nearly jump out of my skin. If I hadn't known it was an owl I'd have run for miles!'

Ben grinned and his face ran into a score of creases and wrinkles.

'Why is it called *Mystery* Moor?' persisted Julian. 'Is it a very old name?'

'When my grandad was a boy it was called *Misty* Moor,' said the old blacksmith, remembering. 'See, *Misty*, not *Mystery*. And that was because of the sea-fogs that came stealing in from the coast, and lay heavy on the moor, so that no man could see his hand in front of his face. Yes, I've been lost in one of those mists, and right scared I was too. It swirled round me like a live thing, and touched me all over with its cold damp fingers.'

'How horrid!' said Anne with a shiver. 'What did you do?'

'Well, first I ran for my life,' said Ben, getting out his pipe and looking into the empty bowl. 'I ran over heather and into gorse. I fell a dozen times, and all the time the mist was feeling me with its damp fingers, trying to get me, that's what the old folk used to say of that mist, it was always trying to get you!'

'Still, it was only a mist,' said George, feeling that the old man was exaggerating. 'Does it still come over the moor?'

'Oh ay,' said Ben, ramming some tobacco into his pipe. 'Autumn's the time, but it comes suddenly at any moment of the year. I've known it come at the end of a fine summer's day, creeping in stealthily, and my, if you don't happen to see it soon enough, it gets you!'

'What do you mean, it *gets* you?' said George.

'Well, it may last for days,' said old Ben. 'And if you're lost on the moors, you're really lost, and you never come back. Ah, smile if you like, young man, but I *know*!' He went off into memories of long ago, looking down at his pipe. 'Let's see now, there was old Mrs Banks, who went bilberry-picking with her basket on a summer's afternoon, and no one ever heard of her again, after the mist came down. And there was young Victor who played truant and went off to the moor, and the mist got him too.'

'I can see we'd better watch out for the mist if we go riding there,' said Dick. 'This is the first I've heard of it.'

'Yes. You keep your eyes skinned,' said old Ben. 'Look away to the coast side and watch there, that's where it comes from. But there aren't many mists nowadays, though I don't know why. No, now I think of it, there hasn't been a mist, not a proper wicked one, for nearly three years.'

'What I'd like to know is why was the name changed to *Mystery* Moor,' said Henry. 'I can understand its being called Misty Moor, but now everyone calls it *Mystery*, not Misty.'

'Well now, that must have been about seventy years ago, when I was a boy,' said Ben, lighting his pipe and puffing hard. He was enjoying himself. He didn't often get such an interested audience as this, five of them, including a dog who sat and listened too!

'That was when the Bartle family built the little railway over the moor,' he began, and stopped at the exclamations of his five listeners.

'Ah! We wanted to know about that!'

'Oh! You know about the railway then?'

'Do go on!'

The blacksmith seemed to get some trouble with his pipe and pulled at it for an exasperatingly long time. George wished she was a horse and could stamp her foot impatiently!

'Well, the Bartle family was a big one,' said Ben at last. 'All boys, but for one ailing little girl. Big strong fellows they were, I remember them well. I was scared of them, they were so free with their fists. Well, one of them, Dan, found a mighty good stretch of sand out there on the moor—'

'Oh yes, we *thought* there might have been a sand-quarry,' said Anne. Ben frowned at the interruption.

'And as there were nine or ten good strong

Bartles, they reckoned to make a fine do of it,' said Ben. 'They got wagons and they went to and from the quarry they dug, and they sold their sand for miles around, good, sharp sand it was . . .'

'We saw some,' said Henry. 'But what about the rails?'

'Don't hurry him,' said Dick, with a frown.

'They made a great deal of money,' said Ben, remembering. 'And they set to work and built a little railway to carry an engine and trucks to the quarry and back, to save labour. My, my, that was a nine days' wonder, that railway! Us youngsters used to follow the little engine, puffing along, and we all longed to drive it. But we never did. Those Bartles kept a big stick, each one of them, and they whipped the hide off any boy that got too near them. Fierce they were, and quarrelsome.'

'Why did the railway fall into ruin?' asked Julian. 'The rails are all overgrown with heather and grass. You can hardly see them.'

'Well, now we come to the Mystery you keep

on about,' said Ben, taking an extra big puff at his pipe. 'Those Bartles fell foul of the travellers up on the moor—'

'Oh, were there travellers on the moor *then*?' said Dick. 'There are some now!'

'Oh ay, there's always been travellers on the moor, long as I can remember,' said the blacksmith. 'Well, it's said those travellers quarrelled with the Bartles, and it wasn't hard to do that, most people did! And the travellers pulled up bits of the line, here and there, and the little engine toppled over and pulled the trucks with it.'

The children could quite well imagine the little engine puffing along, coming to the damaged rails and falling over. What a to-do there must have been up on the moor then!

'The Bartles weren't ones to put up with a thing like that,' said Ben, 'so they set about to drive all the travellers off the moor, and they swore that if so much as one caravan went there, they'd set fire to it and chase the travellers over to the coast and into the sea!'

'They *must* have been a fierce family,' said Anne.

'You're right there,' said Ben. 'All nine or ten of them were big upstanding men, with great shaggy eyebrows that almost hid their eyes, and loud voices. Nobody dared to cross them. If they did, they'd have the whole family on their doorstep with sticks. They ruled this place, they did, and my, they were hated! Us children ran off as soon as we saw one coming round a corner.'

'What about the travellers? Did the Bartles manage to drive them off the moor?' asked George, impatiently.

'Now let me go my own pace,' said Ben, pointing at her with his pipe. 'You want a Bartle after you, young man, that's what you want!' He thought she was a boy, of course. He did something to his pipe and made them all wait a little. Julian winked at the others. He liked this old fellow with his long, long memories.

'Now, you can't cross the travellers for long,'

said Ben, at last. 'That's a fact, you can't. And one day all the Bartles disappeared and never come back home. No, not one of them. All that was left of the family was little lame Agnes, their sister.'

Everyone exclaimed in surprise and old Ben looked round with satisfaction. Ah, he could tell a story, he could!

'But what happened?' said Henry.

'Well, no one rightly knows,' said Ben. 'It happened in a week when the mist came swirling over the moors and blotted everything out. Nobody went up there except the Bartles, and they were safe because all they had to do was to follow their railway lines there and back. They went up to the quarry each day the mist was there, and worked the same as usual. Nothing stopped those Bartles from working!'

He paused and looked round at his listeners. He dropped his voice low, and all five of the children felt little shivers up their backs.

'One night somebody in the village saw twenty or more travellers' caravans slinking through the village at dead of night,' said Ben. 'Up on the moor they went in the thick mist. Maybe they followed the railway; nobody knows. And next morning, up to the quarry went the Bartles as usual, swallowed up in the mist.'

He paused again. 'And they never came back,' he said. 'No, not one of them. Never heard of again!'

'But what *happened*?' said George.

'Search-parties were sent out when the mist cleared,' said old Ben. 'But not one of the Bartles did they find, alive or dead. Not one! And they didn't find any travellers' caravans either. They'd all come creeping back the next night, and passed through the village like shadows. I reckon the travellers set upon the Bartles in the mist that day, fought them and defeated them, and took them and threw them over the cliffs into the roaring sea!'

'How horrible!' said Anne, feeling sick.

'Don't worry yourself!' said the blacksmith. 'It all happened a long time ago, and there weren't many that mourned those Bartles, I can tell you. Funny thing was, their weakly little sister, Agnes, she lived to be a hale old woman of ninety-six, and only died a few years ago! And to think those strong fierce brothers of hers went all together like that!'

'It's a most interesting story, Ben,' said Julian. 'So Misty Moor became *Mystery* Moor then, did it? And nobody ever *really* found out what happened, so the mystery was never solved. Didn't anyone work the railway after that, or get the sand?'

'No, not a soul,' said Ben. 'We were all scared, you see, and young Agnes, she said the railway and the trucks and engine could rot, for all she cared. I never dared to go near them after that. It was a long time before anyone but the travellers set foot on Misty Moor again. Now it's all forgotten, the tale of the Bartles, but those travellers still remember, I've no doubt! They've got good memories, they have.'

'Do you know why they come to Mystery Moor every so often?' asked Dick.

'No. They come and they go,' said Ben. 'They've their own funny ways. They don't belong anywhere, those folk. What they do on the moor is their own business, and I wouldn't want to poke *my* nose into it. I'd remember those old Bartles, and keep away!'

A voice came from inside the smithy, where Jim, the blacksmith's grandson, had been shoeing the horses. 'Grandad! Stop jabbering away there, and let the children come and talk to *me*! I've shod nearly all the horses.'

Ben laughed. 'Go along,' he said to the children. 'I know you'd like to be in there and see the sparks fly, and the shoes made. I've wasted your time, I have, telling you long-ago things. Go along into the smithy. And just remember two things – watch out for that mist, and keep away from the travellers on the moor!'

# [10]

## Sniffer's patrins

It was fun in the smithy, working the bellows, seeing the fire glow, and watching the red-hot shoes being shaped. Jim was quick and clever, and it was a pleasure to watch him.

'Have you been hearing Grandad's old stories?' he said. 'It's all he's got to do now, sit there and remember, though when he wants to he can make a horseshoe as well as I can! There, that's the last one. Stand still, Sultan. That's right!'

The five children were soon on their way back again. It was a lovely morning, and the banks and ditches they passed were bright gold with thousands of celandines.

'All beautifully polished!' said Anne, picking two or three for her button-hole. It *did* look as if someone had polished the inside of each petal, for they gleamed like enamel.

'What a strange tale the old man told,' said Julian. 'He told it well!'

'Yes. He made me feel I don't want to go up on the moor again!' said Anne.

'Don't be feeble!' said George. 'It all happened ages ago. Jolly interesting too. I wonder if the travellers who are there now know the story. Maybe their great-grandparents were the ones who set on the Bartles that misty day!'

'Well, Sniffer's father looked sly enough to carry out a plan like that,' said Henry. 'What about us having a shot at following the way they went, and seeing if we can make out the patrins that Sniffer told George he would leave?'

'Good idea,' said Julian. 'We'll go this afternoon. I say, what's the time? I should think it must be half past lunch-time!'

They looked at their watches. 'Yes, we're late, but we always are when we get back from the blacksmith,' said George. 'Never mind, I bet Mrs Johnson will have an extra special meal for us!'

She had! There was an enormous plate of stew for everyone, complete with carrots, onions, parsnips and turnips, and a date pudding to follow. Good old Mrs Johnson!

'You three girls must wash up for me afterwards,' she said. 'I've such a lot to do today.'

'Why can't the boys help?' said George at once.

'*I'll* do all the washing-up!' said Anne with a sudden grin. 'You four *boys* can go out to the stables!'

Dick gave her a good-natured shove. 'You know we'll help, even if we're not good at it. I'll dry. I hate those bits and pieces that float about in the washing-bowl.'

'Will it be all right if we go up on the moors this afternoon?' asked George.

'Yes, quite all right. But if you want to take your tea, you'll have to pack it yourselves,' said Mrs Johnson. 'I'm taking the small children out for a ride, and there's one on the leading-rein still, as you know.'

They were ready to set off at three o'clock,

their tea packed and everything. The horses were caught in the field and got ready too. They set off happily.

'Now we'll see if we are as clever as we think we are, at reading traveller patrins!' said George. 'Timmy, don't chase *every* rabbit you see, or you'll be left behind!'

They cantered up on to the moor, passing the place where the caravans had stood. They knew the direction they had taken, and here and there they saw wheel-marks. It was fairly easy to follow their trail, because five caravans made quite a path to follow.

'Here's where they camped first,' said Julian, riding up to a blackened spot that showed where a fire had been lit. 'We ought to find a message left somewhere here.'

They searched for one. George found it. 'It's here, behind this tree!' she called. 'Out of the wind.'

They dismounted and came round George. On the ground was the patrin, the shape of a cross, the long stick pointing forwards, in the direction they were going. Other single sticks lay there, to show that a caravan had gone that way, and beside them were the large and the small leaf, weighted with tiny stones.

'What did those leaves show now, oh yes, Sniffer and his dog!' said Dick. 'Well, we're on the right way, though we'd know that anyhow, by the fire!'

They mounted again and went on. It proved quite easy to find and follow the patrins. Only once did they find any difficulty and that was when they came to a place, marked by two trees, where there was no apparent sign in the heather of any caravan marks.

'The heather's so jolly thick here that it's taken the caravans as if it were a feather-bed, springing up when they had gone, and giving no sign of where they had passed,' said Julian. He dismounted and had a good look round. No, there was no sign.

'We'll go on a little way,' he said. 'We may come to a camping place, then we'll know.'

But they came to no old camping place, and

stopped at last in bewilderment. 'We've lost the trail,' said Dick. 'We're not such good travellers after all!'

'Let's go back to those two trees,' said George. 'We can still just see them. If it's so easy to lose the way there, there *might* be a patrin, although there are no camp marks. After all, a patrin is left to show the way, in case the ones following take the wrong route.'

So back they rode to the two trees, and there, sure enough, was Sniffer's patrin! Henry found it set carefully between the trees, so that nothing could disturb it.

'Here's the cross, and the single sticks, and the leaves!' she said. 'But look, the long stick of the cross points to the east and we went off to the north. No wonder we found no signs of the caravans!'

They set off to the east this time, across the thick, springy heather, and almost at once found signs of the passing of caravans: twigs broken off the bushes, a wheel rut on a soft piece of ground.

'We're right now,' said Julian, pleased. 'I was beginning to think it was all too easy for words! But it isn't!'

They rode for two hours, and then decided to have tea. They sat down in a little glade of silver birches, with an unexpected copse of pale primroses behind. Timmy had to make up his mind which to choose, a rabbit chase, or titbits from the children's tea!

He chose both, racing after an imaginary rabbit, and then coming back for a sandwich!

'You know, it's a lot better for us when Mrs Johnson makes sandwiches of tomato or lettuce or something like that,' said Henry. 'We do get them all then, but when we have meat or sardine or egg sandwiches Timmy gets as much as we do!'

'Well, surely you don't mind that, Henrietta,' said George at once. 'You make Timmy sound very greedy. After all, you don't need to give him any of *your* sandwiches!'

'Now, Georgina!' murmured Dick, in her ear.

'Sorry, Georgina,' said Henry, with a grin. 'I just can't *help* giving him a sandwich or two when he comes and sits down and looks at me so longingly.'

'Woof,' said Timmy, and at once sat down in front of Henry, his tongue out, and his eyes fixed unblinkingly on her.

'He sort of *hypnotises* me,' complained Henry. 'Make him go away, George, I shan't be able to keep a single sandwich or bit of cake for myself. Go and stare at someone else, Timmy, for goodness' sake!'

Julian looked at his watch. 'I don't think we ought to spend *too* long over tea,' he said. 'I know we've got summertime now, and the evenings are nice and light, but we haven't reached the travellers' camp yet, and after that we've got to go all the way back. What about starting off again?'

'Right,' said everyone and remounted their horses. They set off through the heather. Soon they found it unexpectedly easy to follow the caravan route, because the soil became sandy, and there were many bare patches on which the marks of the wheels could plainly be seen.

'Goodness, if we go to the east much more, we'll come to the sea!' said Dick.

'No, it's still some miles away,' said Julian. 'Hallo, there's a little hill or something in the distance. First time we've seen anything but complete flatness!'

The wheel-marks led steadily towards the little hill, which, as they came near, seemed to grow considerably bigger. 'I bet the caravans are there,' said George. 'That hill would give a nice bit of shelter from the wind that came from the sea. I believe I can see one!'

George was right. The caravans were there. They showed up well against the hill, in their bright colours.

'They've even got up a washing-line as usual!' said Anne. 'Clothes flapping in the wind!'

'Let's go and ask if Clip is all right,' said Julian. 'It will be a very good excuse for going right up to the camp.'

So they cantered straight up to the little group of five caravans. Four or five men appeared as soon as they heard the sound of hooves. They looked silent and rather forbidding. Sniffer ran out and shouted.

'Hallo! Clip's fine! Quite all right again!'

His father gave him a push and said something sharp to him. He disappeared under the nearest caravan.

Julian rode up to Sniffer's father. 'Did I hear Sniffer say that Clip was quite all right?' he asked. 'Where is he?'

'Over there,' said the man, with a nod of his head. 'No need for you to see him. He's mended fine.'

'All right, all right! I'm not going to take him away from you!' said Julian. 'This is a nice sheltered place you've got, isn't it? How long are you staying?'

'What's that to do with you?' said an old traveller, unpleasantly.

'Nothing,' said Julian, surprised. 'Just a polite question, that's all!'

'How do you get water?' called George. 'Is there a good spring here?'

There was no reply at all. The four or five men had now been joined by others, and there were three mangy-looking dogs growing round. Timmy was beginning to growl back.

'You'd better go before our dogs get you,' said Sniffer's father, sourly.

'Where's Liz?' said George, remembering Sniffer's dog, but before she got an answer the three dogs suddenly made an attack on Timmy! They pounced on him and he had hard work to keep them off. He was far bigger than they were, but they were nippy little things.

'Call off those dogs!' yelled Julian, seeing that George was dismounting to go to Timmy's help. She would get bitten. 'Do you hear me? Call off those dogs.'

Sniffer's father whistled. The three dogs reluctantly left Timmy and went over to the men, their tails down. George had reached Tim and had now got her hand on his collar to stop him from chasing the other three dogs.

'Mount your horse, whistle Timmy, and we'll go,' shouted Julian, not at all liking the silent, sour-looking travellers. George did as she was told. Timmy ran beside her, and they all cantered away from the unpleasant camp.

The men stood watching them in complete silence. 'What's up with them?' said Dick, puzzled. 'Anyone would think they were planning another Bartle affair!'

'Don't!' said Anne. 'They're planning *some*thing, all alone out here, far away from anywhere! I shan't go near them again.'

'They thought we were prying and spying,' said Dick. 'That's all. Poor old Sniffer. What a life he has!'

'We couldn't even tell him that we found his patrins useful,' said George. 'Oh well, there's probably nothing in it, not even an adventure!'

Was she right or wrong? Julian looked at Dick and Dick looked back, his eyebrows raised. They didn't know. Oh well, time would tell!

## [11]

## A nice little plan

The five of them told Captain and Mrs Johnson about their afternoon's experience, as they were having supper.

'Patrins!' said Mrs Johnson. 'So Sniffer told you about those? But I really don't think you should visit the travellers' camp. Those particular travellers are a surly, bad-tempered lot.'

'Did you ever hear the tale of the Big Bartles?' said Henry, getting ready to relate it, and add little bits of her own, here and there!

'No. But it can wait, I'm sure,' said Mrs Johnson, knowing Henry's habit of leaving her food quite uneaten once she began on some marvellous tale. 'Is it one of your tales? You can tell it after supper.'

'It's *not* Henry's tale,' said George, annoyed that Henry should get all the limelight again, and take the blacksmith's tale for her own. 'It's one old Ben told us. Ju, *you* tell it!'

'Nobody is to tell it *now*,' said Captain Johnson. 'You came in late for supper, we waited for you, and the least you can do is to get on with your eating.'

The five juniors at the other table were disappointed. They had hoped to hear another of Henry's marvellous stories. But Captain Johnson was hungry and tired.

'Old Ben is a great age, as you said,' began Henry, after a few mouthfuls. 'He—'

'Not another word, please, Henrietta,' said the captain, curtly. Henry went red and George grinned, kicking at Dick under the table. Unfortunately she kicked Henry instead, and the girl glared at her for a whole minute.

'Oh dear!' thought Anne. 'Just as we'd had such a lovely day! I suppose we're all tired and scratchy.'

'*Why* did you kick me?' began Henry in a cross voice, as soon as she and George left the table with the others.

'Shut up, you two,' said Julian. 'She probably meant to kick me or Dick, not you.'

Henry shut up. She didn't like Julian to tick her off. George looked mutinous and went off with Timmy.

Dick yawned. 'What jobs are there to do, if any?' he said. 'Don't say there's washing-up again. I feel I might break a few things.'

Mrs Johnson heard him and laughed. 'No, there's no washing-up. The woman has come in to do it tonight. Have a look at the horses – and see that Jenny the mare is not with Flash, you know she doesn't like her for some reason, and *will* kick out at her. She must always be kept in another field.'

'That's all right, Mrs Johnson,' said William, suddenly appearing, stolid and competent as ever. 'I've seen to that. I've seen to everything, really.'

'You're better than any stable boy, William,' said Mrs Johnson, smiling at him. 'I wish you'd take a permanent job here!'

'I wish you meant that,' said William, earnestly. There was nothing he would have liked better! He went off looking pleased.

'I think you'd better all go to bed then, as William appears to have done everything necessary,' said Mrs Johnson. 'Any plans for tomorrow?'

'Not yet,' said Julian, trying to stop a yawn. 'So if you want anything done, we'll do it.'

'We'll see what tomorrow brings,' said Mrs Johnson and said good night. The boys said good night to the three girls and went off to the stable.

'Gosh, we've forgotten to undress and wash and everything,' said Julian, half-asleep. 'What's the matter with us at this place? I can't seem to keep my eyes open after half past eight!'

The next day certainly brought a few things. It brought a letter for Henry that filled her with disgust. It brought two letters for Mrs Johnson that made her start fussing and worrying. It brought a letter for Captain Johnson that sent him down to the station at once.

Henrietta's letter was from two of her great-aunts. They announced that as they would be near the stables that day and the following, they would like to fetch her and take her out with them.

'Blow!' said Henrietta, ungratefully. 'Great-Aunts Hannah and Lucy *would* choose this very week to come along and see me! Just when Julian and Dick are here, and everything is such fun. Can't I phone and say I'm too busy, Mrs Johnson?'

'Certainly not,' said Mrs Johnson, shocked. 'That would be very rude, Henry, and you know it. You're having the whole of the Easter holidays here, and yet you think you can't spare two days. As a matter of fact I shall be glad if your aunts *do* take you off my hands for a couple of days.'

'Why?' asked Henry, astonished. 'Have I been a nuisance?'

'Oh no, but I've had two letters this morning telling me that four children are coming un-expectedly,' said Mrs Johnson. 'They were not supposed to come till three of the others left this weekend, but there you are! These things happen. *Where* I am to put them I really don't know!'

'Oh dear!' said Anne. 'Do you think Dick and Julian ought to go home, Mrs Johnson? You didn't plan for them, you know, they just came.'

'Yes, I know,' said Mrs Johnson. 'But we're more or less used to that, and I do like having bigger boys, I must say, they're such a help. Now let me see. What *can* we do?'

Captain Johnson came in, looking hurried. 'I've just had a letter, dear,' he said. 'I've got to go down to the station. Those two new horses have arrived. Two days before I wanted them – what a nuisance!'

'This is one of those *days*!' said Mrs Johnson, desperately. 'Good gracious, how many shall we be in the house? And however many horses shall we have? No, I can't count this morning. I'm all muddle-headed!'

Anne felt that it was a pity that she and George and the boys couldn't immediately pack and go home. After all, poor Mrs Johnson had thought that she and George *would* have gone home three or four days ago, and instead of that they had stayed on and the boys had arrived as well!

Anne hurried to find Julian. He would know what to do. She found him with Dick, carrying straw for the stables.

'Julian! Listen! I want to talk to you,' said Anne. Julian let the load of straw slip to the ground, and turned to Anne.

'What's up?' he said. '*Don't* tell me it's a row between George and Henry again, because I shan't listen!'

'No. Nothing like that,' said Anne. 'It's Mrs Johnson. She's got four children coming unexpectedly, before the others go. She's in a great state about it, and I wondered what we could do to help. You see, she didn't expect any of *us* four to be here this week.'

'No. That's true,' said Julian, sitting down on his straw. 'Let's think hard.'

'It's easy!' said Dick. 'We'll simply take our

tents, some food, and go and camp out on the moor by some spring. WHAT could be nicer?'

'Oh *yes*!' said Anne, her eyes shining. 'Oh Dick that's a *marvellous* idea! Mrs Johnson will get rid of us all and Timmy too, then, and we would have a lovely time all by ourselves!'

'Killing quite a lot of birds with one stone!' said Julian. 'We've got a couple of tents in our kit, Anne. Very small ones, but they'll do. And we can borrow rubber sheets to put on the heather, though it's as dry as a bone, as far as I can see!'

'I'll go and tell George!' said Anne, joyfully. 'Let's go today, Julian, and be out of the way before the new children come. Captain Johnson's got two new horses coming too. He'll be very glad to have a few of us out of the way!'

She flew off to tell George. George was busy polishing some harness, a job she liked very much. She listened to Anne's excited tale. Henry was there too, looking gloomy. She looked gloomier still at the end.

'It's too bad,' she said, when Anne had

finished. 'I could have come with you if it hadn't been for these great-aunts of mine. *WHY* did they have to come just at this very moment? Don't you think it's maddening?'

Neither Anne nor George thought it was maddening. They were secretly very pleased indeed to think that they could once more go off entirely on their own, with Timmy, as they had so often done before. But they would have *had* to ask Henry if her aunts hadn't written at this very lucky moment!

George didn't like to show how delighted she was to think of going off camping on the moor. She and Anne did a little comforting of poor Henry and then went off to make arrangements with Mrs Johnson.

'Well, that's a very bright idea of Dick's!' she said in delight. 'It solves a whole lot of problems. And I know you don't mind. You're thrilled at the chance, aren't you! It's really very helpful. I only wish poor Henry could go too, but she *must* go out with her old great-aunts. They adore her!'

'Of course she must,' said George, solemnly. She and Anne exchanged a look. Poor Henry! But really, it would be very nice to be without her for a little while.

Everyone began to be suddenly very busy. Dick and Julian undid their packs to find out exactly what was in them. Mrs Johnson looked out rubber sheets and old rugs. She was a wonder at producing things like that!

William wanted to go with them and help to carry the things, but nobody wanted his help. They just wanted to be off and away by themselves, just the Five and nobody else! Timmy caught the excitement too and his tail thumped and wagged the whole morning.

'You'll be pretty well loaded,' said Mrs Johnson, doubtfully. 'It's a good thing that fine weather is forecast, or you'd have to take macs as well. Still, I imagine you won't go very far on the moors, will you? You can easily get back to the stable if you have forgotten anything, or want more food.'

They were ready at last, and went to find

Henry to say good-bye. She stared at them mournfully. She had changed into a smart little coat and dress. She looked completely different and very gloomy.

'What part of the moor are you going to?' she asked eagerly. 'Up the railway?'

'Yes. We thought we would,' said Julian. 'Just to see where it goes to. And it's a nice straight way to follow. We can't lose our way if we keep near the railway!'

'Have a good time, Henry,' said George, with a grin. 'Do they call you Henrietta?'

'Yes,' said poor Henry, putting on a pair of gloves. 'Well, good-bye. For goodness' sake don't stay away too long. Thank goodness you're all such a hungry lot. You'll simply have to come back and get more food in a couple of days!'

They grinned and left her, Timmy at their heels. They made their way to the moor, intending to cut out the part of the railway that ran to Milling Green, and join it some way before that.

'Now we're off,' said George, contentedly. 'Without that chatterbox of a Henry.'

'She's *really* not too bad,' said Dick. 'All the same, it's fine to be on our own, just the Famous Five together!'

# [12]

## The little railway

It was a very hot day. The five had had their lunch before they started, as Mrs Johnson said it would be easier to carry that inside than outside!

Even Timmy carried something. George said that he ought to do his share, and had neatly fastened a bag of his pet biscuits on his back.

'There now!' she said. 'You've got your load too. No, don't try and sniff the biscuits all the time, Timmy. You can't walk with your head screwing round like that. You ought to be used to the smell of biscuits by this time!'

They set off to the railway line, or where they hoped it would be. It took a little time to discover it running under the heather. Julian was glad. He didn't want to walk right into Milling Green to find the beginning of it and then walk all the way up again!

Anne found it by tripping over it! 'Oh!' she said. 'Here it is! I caught my foot in a bit of rusty line. Look, you can hardly see it!'

'Good,' said Julian, and stepped in between the narrow pair of old, rusty lines. In some places they had rusted away, and there were gaps. In other places the heather had grown completely over the lines, and unless the children had known that they must keep straight forward, they would have lost them completely. As it was they sometimes missed them and once had to do quite a bit of scrabbling about in the heather to see if they could feel them.

It was very hot. Their packs began to feel distinctly heavy. Timmy's biscuits began to slide round his body and eventually hung below his tummy. He didn't like that, and George suddenly spied him sitting down trying to prise open the bag with his teeth!

She put down her own pack and adjusted Timmy's. 'If only you didn't keep chasing rabbits, and making your pack swing about, it wouldn't slip,' she said. 'There now, it's all right again, Tim. Walk to heel and it won't slip any more.'

They went on and on up the railway lines. Sometimes the rails took a curve round an unexpected rock. Soon the soil began to look sandy, and the heather did not grow so thickly. It was easier to see the lines, though in some places the sand had sifted over them and hidden them.

'I really *must* have a rest!' said Anne, sitting down in some heather. 'I feel I want to pant and hang my tongue out like Timmy!'

'I wonder how far these lines go,' said Dick. 'It's so very sandy now underfoot that I feel we must be getting near the quarry!'

They lay back in the heather and felt very sleepy. Julian yawned and sat up.

'This really won't do!' he said. 'If we fall asleep we'll never want to start off with our heavy packs again. Stir yourselves, lazy-bones!'

They all got up again. Timmy's biscuits had slithered round to his tummy once more, and George had to put them right again. Timmy stood quietly, panting, his tongue hanging out. He thought the biscuits were a great nuisance. It would be much easier to eat them!

The sand got deeper and soon there were big sandy patches with no heather or grass at all. The wind blew the sand up in the air, and the five found that they had to shut their eyes against it.

'I say! The lines end here!' said Julian, stopping suddenly. 'Look, they're broken, wrenched out of place, the engine couldn't go any farther.'

'They may appear again a bit farther on,' said Dick, and went to look. But he couldn't find any, and came back to look at the lines again.

'It's funny,' he said. 'We aren't at any quarry yet, are we? I quite thought that the line would run right to the quarry, the trucks would fill up there, and the engine would pull them back to Milling Green. *Where* is the quarry? Why do the lines stop so suddenly here?'

'Yes. The quarry *should* be near here,

shouldn't it?' said Julian. 'Well, there simply must be more lines somewhere! Ones that go to the quarry. Let's look for the quarry first, though. We ought to see that easily enough!'

But it wasn't really very easy to find because it was behind a great mass of thick tall gorse bushes. Dick rounded them and stopped. Behind the enormous spread of bushes was a great pit, a sandy pit quarried and hollowed for its beautiful sand.

'Here it is!' called Dick. 'Come and look! My word, there's been some quarrying here for sand. They must have taken tons and tons out of it!'

The others came to look. It certainly was an enormous pit, deep and wide. They put their packs beside it and leapt down. Their feet sank into the fine sand.

'The sides are pitted with holes,' said Dick. 'I bet hundreds of sand-martins nest here in May!'

'There are even some caves,' said George, in surprise. 'Sand caves! Well, we can easily shelter here if we have rain. Some of these caves seem to go quite a long way back.'

'Yes. But I'd be a bit afraid of the sand falling in and burying me, if I crawled in,' said Anne. 'It's quite loose, look!' She scraped some down with her hand.

'I've found the lines!' called Julian. 'Here, look. The sand has almost covered them. I trod on a rail and it was so rotten it broke beneath my foot!'

The others went to see, Timmy too. He was quite delighted with this place. The rabbit holes in it! What fun he was going to have!

'Let's follow these lines,' said Julian. So they kicked away the sand from the rails and followed them slowly out of the quarry and towards the ends of the other broken lines.

About ten yards from these the lines they were following were wrenched apart. Some were flung into the nearby heather, and could be seen there, bent and rusty.

The children stared at them. 'I guess the travellers did that, when the Bartles were here years ago,' said Dick. 'The day they attacked them perhaps. I say, look, what*ever's* that great lump over there, with gorse growing over it?'

They went to see. Timmy saw the lump and couldn't make it out. He growled warningly at it.

Julian took up a broken piece of rail and forced back the gorse bush that had grown over and around the great lump, almost hiding it.

'See what it is?' he said, startled.

They all stared. 'Why, it's the engine! The little engine old Ben the blacksmith told us about!' said Dick. 'It must have run right off the broken lines and overturned here, and through the years these great gorse bushes grew up and hid it. Poor old engine!'

Julian forced the gorse back a little more. 'What a funny old-fashioned affair!' he said. 'Look at the funnel, and the fat little boiler. And see, there's the small cab. It can't have had much more power, only just enough to puff along with a few trucks!'

'What happened to the trucks?' wondered Anne.

'Well, they would be easy enough to set upright again and put on the rails, and hand-pushed to Milling Green,' said Dick. 'But this engine couldn't be lifted, except by some kind of machinery. Not even a dozen men could lift it and set it on the rails!'

'The travellers must have set on the Bartles in the mist, having first broken up the lines so that the engine would run off and overturn,' said Julian. 'They may even have used the broken rails to attack them with. Anyway, they won the battle, because not one of the Bartles ever returned.'

'Some of the villagers must have gone to see what became of them and have got the trucks back on the lines and pushed them to Milling Green,' said George, trying to reconstruct the long-ago happenings in her mind. 'But they couldn't do anything about the engine.'

'That's about it,' said Julian. 'My word, what a shock for the Bartles when they saw the travellers creeping out at them from the mist, like shadows!'

'I hope we don't dream about this tonight,' said Anne.

They went back to the quarry. 'This wouldn't be a bad place to camp in,' said Dick. 'The sand is so dry and so soft. We could make lovely beds for ourselves. We wouldn't need the tents up, either, because the sides of the quarry shelter us beautifully from the wind.'

'Yes. Let's camp here,' said Anne, pleased. 'There are quite a lot of nice holes to store our things in.'

'What about water?' asked George. 'We want to be fairly near it, don't we? Timmy, find some water! Drink, Timmy, drink! Aren't you thirsty? Your tongue looks as if it is, the way you are hanging it out like a flag!'

Timmy put his head on one side as George talked to him. Water? Drink? He knew what both those words meant! He ran off, sniffing the air. George watched him.

He disappeared round a bush and was away for about half a minute. When he came back George gave a pleased shout.

'He's found some water! Look – his mouth is all wet! Timmy, where is it?'

Timmy wagged his tail vigorously, glad that George was pleased with him. He ran round the bush again and the others followed.

He led them to a little green patch and stopped. A spring bubbled up like a small fountain, dancing a little in the sunshine. The water fell from it into a little channel it had made for itself in the sand, ran away for a short distance, and then disappeared underground again.

'Thank you, Tim,' said George. 'Julian, is the water all right to drink here?'

'Well, I can see some that *is*!' said Julian, pointing to the right. 'The Bartles must have put a pipe in that bank, look, and caught another spring there, a much bigger one. It's as clear as can be. That will do fine for us!'

'Good,' said Anne, pleased. 'It's hardly any way from the quarry. It's as cold as ice, too – feel!'

They felt, and then they drank from their

palms. How cold and pure! The moor must be full of these little bubbling springs, welling up from underground. That explained the brilliant green patches here and there.

'Now let's sit down and have some tea,' said Anne, unpacking the bag she had carried. 'It's too hot to feel really hungry.'

'Oh no, it isn't,' said Dick. 'Speak for your-self, Anne!'

They sat in the sunny quarry, the sand warm to their legs. 'Far away from anybody!' said Anne, pleased. 'Nobody near us for miles!'

But she wasn't quite right. There was some-body much nearer than she thought!

# [13]

# A noise in the night

It was Timmy who first knew there was some-body not far off. He pricked up his ears and listened. George saw him.

'What is it, Tim?' she said. 'Nobody is com-ing here, surely?'

Timmy gave a tiny growl, as if he were not quite sure of himself. Then he leapt up, his tail wagging, and tore out of the quarry!

'Where's he gone to?' said George, aston-ished. 'Gosh, here he is, back again!'

So he was, and with him was a funny little hearth-rug of a dog – yes, Liz! She was not quite sure of her welcome and crawled up to the children on her tummy, looking more like a hearth-rug than ever!

Timmy leapt round her in delight. She might have been his very best friend, he was so delighted! George patted the funny little dog and Julian looked thoughtful.

'I hope this doesn't mean that we are anywhere near the travellers' camp,' he said. 'It's quite likely that the lines might end somewhere near them. I've rather lost my sense of direction.'

'Oh goodness, I do HOPE we're not near their camp!' said Anne, in dismay. 'Those old-time travellers must have camped pretty near to the Bartles' quarry before they attacked them, so perhaps the present camp is near too.'

'Well, what's it matter if it is?' said Dick. 'Who's afraid of them? *I'm* not!'

They all sat still, thinking hard, Liz licking Anne's hand. And in the silence they heard an all-too-familiar sound.

Sniff! Sniff!

'Sniffer!' called George. 'Come on out, wherever you are hiding. I can hear you!'

A pair of legs stuck out from a great clump of heather at the edge of the quarry, and then the whole of Sniffer's wiry little body slithered out and down into the sand. He sat there, grinning at them, half-afraid to come any nearer in case they were cross with him.

'What are *you* doing here?' said Dick. 'Not spying on us, I hope?'

'No,' said Sniffer. 'Our camp isn't very far away. Liz heard you, I think, and ran off. I followed her.'

'Oh blow. We hoped we weren't near anyone else,' said George. 'Does anyone at your camp know we're here?'

'Not yet,' said Sniffer. 'But they'll find out. They always do. I won't tell, though, if you don't want me to.'

Dick tossed him a biscuit. 'Well, keep your mouth shut if you can,' he said. 'We're not interfering with anyone and we don't want anyone interfering with us. See?'

Sniffer nodded. He suddenly put his hand in his pocket and pulled out the red and white hanky that George had given him. It was still clean and beautifully folded.

'Not dirty yet!' he said to George.

'Well, it ought to be,' said George. 'It's for your sniffs. No, *don't* use your coat-sleeve.'

Sniffer simply could *not* understand why he should use a beautiful clean hanky when he had a dirty coat-sleeve. He put the hanky carefully back into his pocket.

Liz ran to him and fawned on him. Sniffer fondled the peculiar little creature, and then Timmy went over and played with them both. The four finished their tea, threw Sniffer one last biscuit, and got up to put their things away safely. Now that Sniffer was about, and the travellers' camp near, they didn't feel it was terribly safe to leave anything unguarded or unhidden.

'Scoot off, now, Sniffer,' said Julian. 'And no spying on us, mind! Timmy will know immediately you arrive anywhere near, and come hunting for you. If you want to see us, give a whistle when you get near. No creeping or slipping into the quarry. Understand?'

'Yes,' said Sniffer, standing up. He took the hanky from his pocket again, waved it at George, and disappeared with Liz at his heels.

'I'm just going to see exactly how near to the travellers' camp we are,' Julian said. He walked to the entrance of the quarry and up on to the moor. He looked in the direction that Sniffer had gone. Yes, there was the hill in the shelter of which the travellers had their caravans. It wasn't more than a quarter of a mile away. Blow! Still, it was far enough for the travellers not to discover them, unless by chance.

'Or unless Sniffer gives the game away,' thought Julian. 'Well, we'll spend the night here, anyway, and we can move off somewhere else tomorrow if we feel like it.'

They felt rather energetic that evening and played a ball game in the quarry, in which Timmy joined wholeheartedly. But as he always got the ball before anyone else did they had to tie him up in order to get a game themselves. Timmy was very cross. He turned his back on them and sulked.

'He looks like you now, George,' said Dick, grinning, and got the ball bang on the side of his head from an angry George!

Nobody wanted much supper. Julian took a little aluminium jug to the spring and filled it once for everyone. It really was lovely water from that bubbling spring!

'I wonder how Henry's getting on,' said Anne. 'Spoilt to bits by her great-aunts, I expect. Didn't she look odd in proper clothes!'

'Yes, she ought to have been a boy,' said Dick. 'Like you, George,' he added hastily. 'Both of you are real sports, plucky as anything.'

'How do you know Henry's plucky?' said George, scornfully. 'Only by her silly tales! I bet they're all made up and exaggerated.'

Julian changed the subject. 'Shall we want rugs tonight, do you think?' he said.

'You bet! It may be warm now, and the sand is hot with the sun, but it won't be quite so nice when it's gone down,' said Anne. 'Anyway we can always creep into one of those cosy little caves if we feel chilly. They're as warm as toast. I went into one, so I know.'

They settled down quite early to sleep. The

boys took one side of the quarry, the girls the other. Tim, as usual, was on George's feet, much to Anne's discomfort.

'He's on mine too,' she complained to George. 'He's *so long*, he stretches over my feet as well. Move him, George.'

So George moved him, but as soon as Anne was asleep he stretched out again and lay on both girls' legs. He slept with one ear open.

He heard a scurrying hedgehog. He heard all the rabbits out for a night-time game. He heard the frogs in a far-off pool croaking in the night. His sharp ear even heard the tinkle of the little spring outside the pit.

Nobody moved in the quarry. There was a small moon but it gave very little light. The stars that studded the sky seemed to give more light than the moon.

Timmy's one open ear suddenly pricked itself right up. Then the other ear stood up too. Timmy was still asleep but his ears were both listening very hard!

A low, humming sound came slowly over the

night. It came nearer and nearer. Timmy awoke
properly and sat up, listening, his eyes wide
open now.

The sound was now very loud indeed. Dick
awoke and listened. What *was* that noise? An
aeroplane? It must be jolly low! Surely it wasn't
about to land on the moor in the dark!

He woke Julian and they both got up and
went out of the quarry. 'It's an aeroplane all
right,' said Dick, in a low voice. 'What's it
doing? It doesn't seem to be going to land. It's
gone round in a low circle two or three times.'

'Is it in trouble, do you think?' asked Julian.
'Here it comes again.'

'Look, what's that light over there?' suddenly
said Dick, pointing to the east. 'See, that sort of
glow. It's not very far from the travellers' camp.'

'I don't know,' said Julian, puzzled. 'It's not a
fire, is it? We can't see any flames and it doesn't
seem to flicker like a fire would.'

'I think it may be some sort of guide to that
plane,' said Dick. 'It seems to be circling round
and about over the glow. Let's watch it.'

They watched it. Yes, it did seem to be circling round the glow, whatever it was, and then, quite suddenly it rose in the air, circled round once more and made off to the east.

'There it goes,' said Dick, straining his eyes. 'I can't tell what kind it is, except that it's very small.'

'What can it have been doing?' said Julian, puzzled. 'I thought the glow might have been to guide it in landing, though where it could land here in safety I simply don't know. But it didn't land at all, it just circled and made off.'

'Where would it have come from?' said Dick. 'From the coast, I suppose, from over the sea, do you think?'

'I simply don't know,' said Julian. 'It beats me! And why should the travellers have anything to do with it? Travellers and planes don't seem to mix, somehow.'

'Well, we don't know that they do have anything to do with the plane, except that we saw that glow,' said Dick. 'And that's going now, look.'

Even as they watched, the bright glow died completely away. Now the moor lay in darkness again.

'Funny,' said Julian, scratching his head. 'I can't make it out. It's true that the travellers may be up to something, the way they come out here secretly, apparently for no purpose at all, and also they don't want us snooping round, that's clear.'

'I think we'd better try and find out what that glow is,' said Dick. 'We could have a bit of a snoop tomorrow. Or perhaps Sniffer could tell us.'

'He might,' said Julian. 'We'll try him. Come on, let's get back into the quarry. It's cold out here!'

The quarry felt quite warm to them as they went down into it. The girls were sound asleep still. Timmy, who had been with them, did not wake them. He had been as puzzled as Julian and Dick over the low-flying plane, but he had not barked at all. Julian had been glad about that, Timmy's bark might have carried right over to the travellers' camp and warned them that someone was camping near.

They got back under their rug, keeping close to one another for warmth. But they soon lost their shivers, and Dick threw off his share of the rug. In a few minutes they were asleep.

Timmy awoke first and stretched himself out in the warm morning sunshine. Anne sat up with a little scream. 'Oh Timmy, *don't*! You nearly squashed me to bits. Do that to George if you must stretch yourself all over somebody!'

The boys awoke then, and went to the spring to splash their faces and bring back a jugful of water to drink. Anne got the breakfast, and over it the boys told the girls of the aeroplane in the night.

'How strange!' said Anne. 'And that glow too. It must have been a guide of some sort to the plane. Let's go and see where it was. It must have been a fire of *some* kind!'

'Right,' said Dick. 'I vote we go this morning, but we'll take Tim with us in case we meet those travellers!'

# The travellers are not pleased

Julian and Dick went to stand where they had stood the night before, trying to see exactly in what direction the glow had been.

'I *think* it was beyond the travellers' camp, to the left,' said Julian. 'What do you think, Dick?'

'Yes. That's about it,' said Dick. 'Shall we go now?' He raised his voice. 'We're going, George and Anne. Are you coming? We can leave our stuff here, tucked away in the caves because we shan't be very long.'

George called back. 'Julian, I think Timmy's got a thorn in his foot or something. He's limping. Anne and I think we'll stay here with him and try to get it out. You go, but for goodness' sake don't get into trouble with the travellers!'

'We shan't,' said Julian. 'We've as much right

on this moor as they have and they know it. All right, we'll leave you two here then with Timmy. Sure you don't want any help with his paw?'

'Oh no,' said George. 'I can manage, thank you.'

The two boys went off, leaving Anne and George fussing over Timmy's paw. He had leapt into a gorse bush after a rabbit and a thorn had gone right into his left fore-paw. Then it had broken off, leaving the point in poor Timmy's pad. No wonder he limped. George was going to have quite a time trying to ease out the bit of thorn.

Julian and Dick set off over the moor. It was a day like summer, far too warm for April. There was not a single cloud to be seen in the sky, which was as blue as forget-me-nots. The boys felt too hot in their pullovers and longed to take them off. But that would mean carrying them, which would be an awful nuisance.

The travellers' camp was not really far away. They soon came near to the curious hill that stood up from the flatness of the moor. The caravans still stood in its shelter, and the boys saw that a little group of men were sitting together, talking earnestly.

'I bet they're having a jaw about that aeroplane last night,' said Dick. 'And I bet it was they who set the light or fire, or whatever it was, to guide it. I wonder why it didn't land.'

They kept in the shelter of big gorse bushes, as they skirted the camp. They were not particularly anxious to be seen. The dogs, sitting round the group of men, apparently did not see or hear them, which was lucky.

The boys made their way towards the place where they thought they had seen the glow, some way to the left of the camp, and beyond it.

'Doesn't seem to be anything out of the ordinary anywhere,' said Julian, stopping and looking round. 'I was expecting to see a big burnt patch, or something.'

'Wait – what's in that dip over there?' said Dick, pointing to where the ground seemed to dip downwards. 'It looks like another old quarry, rather like the one we're camping in, but smaller, much smaller. I bet that's where the fire was!'

They made their way to the quarry. It was much more overgrown than theirs was, and was evidently one that had been worked at an earlier time. It dipped down to quite a pit in the middle and set there was something unusual. What was it?

The boys scrambled down into the pit-like quarry and made their way to the middle. They stared at the big thing that was set there, pointing to the sky.

'It's a lamp, a powerful lamp of some kind,' said Julian. 'Like those we see making a flare-path at an aerodrome, guiding planes in to land. Fancy seeing one here!'

'How did the travellers get it?' wondered Dick, puzzled. 'And why signal to a plane that doesn't land? It looked as if it wanted to, circling round low like that.'

'Maybe the travellers signalled that it wasn't safe to land for some reason,' said Julian. 'Or perhaps they were going to give something to the pilot and it wasn't ready.'

'Well, it's a puzzle,' said Dick. 'I can't *imagine* what's going on. Something is, that's certain. Let's snoop round a bit.'

They found nothing else, except a trail that led to the lamp and back. Just as they were examining it, a shout came to their ears. They swung round – and saw the figure of a traveller at the edge of the pit.

'What are you doing here?' he shouted, in a harsh voice. He was joined by a few others, and they all looked threateningly at Julian and Dick as they climbed out of the pit.

Julian decided to be honest. 'We're camping out on the moor for a night or two,' he said, 'and we heard a plane last night, circling low. We also saw a glow that appeared to be guiding it, and we came along to see what it was. Did *you* hear the plane?'

'Maybe we did and maybe we didn't,' said the nearest traveller, who was Sniffer's father. 'What of it? Planes fly over this moor any day!'

'We found that powerful lamp,' said Dick, pointing back at it. 'Do you know anything about *that*?'

'Nothing,' said the traveller, scowling. 'What lamp?'

'Well, as far as I can see there's no charge for looking at it,' said Julian. 'Go and have a squint, if you don't know anything about it! But I can't believe that you didn't see the light it gave last night! It's a jolly good place to hide it, I must say.'

'We don't know anything about any lamp,' said another traveller, the old one with grey hair. 'This is our usual camping place. We don't interfere with anything or anybody – unless they interfere with us. Then we make them sorry for it.'

The boys at once thought of the long-ago mystery of the disappearance of the Bartles. They felt quite uncomfortable.

'Well, we're going now, so don't worry,' said Julian. 'We're only camping for a night or two, as I said. We won't come near here again, if you object to us.'

He saw Sniffer creeping up behind the men, with Liz, who for some reason of her own, was walking sedately on her hind-legs. Sniffer pulled at his father's arm.

'They're all right,' he said. 'You know our Clip got his leg made better at the stables. They're all right!'

All he got was a savage cuff that sent him to the ground, where he rolled over and over. Liz dropped down on all fours and went to lick him.

'Hey!' said Julian, shocked. 'Leave that kid alone! You've no right to hit him like that!'

Sniffer set up such a yelling that some of the women left the caravans not far off and came running to see what was up. One of them began to shout at Sniffer's father and he shouted back. Soon there was quite a row going on between the men and the angry women, one of whom had picked up poor Sniffer and was dabbing his head with a wet cloth.

'Come on, it's a good time to go,' said Julian to Dick. 'What an unfriendly lot they are, except poor Sniffer, and he was doing his best for us, poor kid.'

The two boys went off quickly, glad to be away from the men and their dogs. They were puzzled about everything. The men said they knew nothing about the lamp, but they *must* know something about it. Nobody but a traveller could have lit it last night.

They went back to the girls and told them what had happened. 'Let's get back to the stables,' said Anne. 'There's something funny going on. We'll be in the middle of an adventure before we know where we are!'

'We'll stay one more night,' said Julian. 'I want to see if that plane comes again. Those travellers don't know where we're camping and though Sniffer knows, I'm pretty sure he won't tell. It was plucky of him to try and stick up for us to his father.'

'All right. We'll stay,' said George. 'I'm not particularly anxious for Timmy to have that long walk home today. I *think* I've got most of that thorn out of his pad, but he still won't put his foot to the ground.'

'He's jolly clever at running about on three legs,' said Dick, watching Timmy tearing round the quarry, sniffing as usual for rabbits.

'The amount of quarrying that Timmy has done in this pit already is colossal!' said Julian, staring round at the places where Timmy had tried to get in at some rabbit hole and scrabbled out big heaps of sand. 'He would have been a great help to the Bartles when they dug out sand! Poor old Tim – your bad foot has stopped you scraping for rabbits, hasn't it!'

Timmy ran over on three legs. He enjoyed all the fussing he got when anything happened to him. He meant to make the most of his bad foot!

They had a very lazy day indeed. It really was too hot to do anything much. They went to the little spring and sat with their feet in the rivulet it made – it was deliciously cool! They went and had a look at the old engine again, lying on its side, half-buried.

Dick scraped away a lot of the sand that had seeped into the cab. Soon they were all helping. They uncovered the old handles and levers and tried to move them. But they couldn't of course.

'Let's go round to the other side of the gorse bush and see if we can see the funnel again,' said Dick, at last. 'Blow these thorns. I'm getting pricked all over. Timmy's very sensible, sitting there, not attempting to examine this old Puffing Billy!'

They had to cut away some of the gorse before they could examine the funnel properly. Then they exclaimed in wonder.

'Look! It's very like the long funnel that Puffing Billy had, you know, one of the first engines ever made!'

'It's filled with sand,' said Dick, and tried to scrape it out. It was fairly loose, and soon he was able to peer down the funnel quite a long way.

'Funny to think of smoke puffing out of this strange old funnel,' said Dick. 'Poor old engine, lying here for years, quite forgotten. I'd have thought *someone* would rescue it!'

'Well, you know what the blacksmith told us,' said George. 'The Bartle sister that was left wouldn't have anything more to do with the railway or the engine or the quarry. And certainly nobody could move this great thing on their own.'

'I shouldn't be surprised if we're the only people in the world who know where the old engine is,' said Anne. 'It's so overgrown that nobody could see it except by accident!'

'I feel jolly hungry, all of a sudden,' said Dick, stopping his work of getting sand off the engine. 'What about something to eat?'

'We've got enough to last for a day or two more,' said Anne. 'Then we'll have to get something else – or go back to the stables.'

'I *must* spend one more night here,' said Julian. 'I want to see if that plane returns again.'

'Right. We'll all watch this time,' said George. 'It will be fun. Come on, let's go and get something to eat. Don't you think that's a good idea, Timmy?'

Timmy certainly did. He limped off at top speed on three legs, though really his left forepaw no longer hurt him. Timmy, you're a fraud!

## [15]

## *A startling night*

No travellers came near them that day, not even Sniffer. The evening was as lovely as the day had been, and almost as warm.

'It's extraordinary!' said Dick, looking up into the sky. 'What weather for April! The bluebells will be rushing out soon if the sun goes on being as hot as this!'

They lay on the sand in the quarry and watched the evening star shine in the sky. It looked very big and bright and round.

Timmy scrabbled round in the sand. 'His paw is much better,' said George. 'Though I notice that he still sometimes holds it up.'

'Only when he wants you to say "Poor Timmy, does it hurt?"' said Dick. 'He's a baby, likes to be fussed!'

They talked for a while and then Anne

yawned. 'It's early, I know – but I believe I'm going to sleep.'

There was soon a trek to the spring, and everyone sluiced themselves in the cool water. There was only one towel between them, but that did very well. Then they settled down in their sandy beds. The sand was beautifully warm and they did not bother about putting down the rubber sheets. There could not possibly be any dampness in that quarry after it had been baked so much by the hot sun!

'I hope we wake when the plane comes, if it does come,' said Julian to Dick, as they lay without any covering in their soft, sandy bed. 'My goodness, isn't it hot! No wonder Timmy's panting over there!'

They went to sleep at last, but Dick awoke suddenly, feeling much too hot. Phew! What a night! He lay looking up at the brilliant stars, and then shut his eyes again. But it was no use, he couldn't go to sleep.

He sat up cautiously, so as not to awake Julian. I think I'll just go and have a squint to see if that big lamp is lit again, down in that pit by the travellers' camp, he thought.

He went to the edge of the quarry and climbed up. He looked towards the travellers' camp and gave a sudden exclamation. Yes! he thought. It's glowing again! I can't see the lamp, of course, but its light is so powerful that I can easily see the glow it makes. It must be very bright, looked down on from the sky. I wonder if the plane is due to come now that the lamp is lit.

He listened, and yes, he could distinctly hear a low humming noise from the east. It must be the plane coming again! Would it land this time, and if so, who was in it?

He ran to wake Julian and the girls. Timmy was alert at once, wagging his tail excitedly. He was always ready for anything, even in the middle of the night! Anne and George got up too, very thrilled.

'Is the lamp really alight again? And I can hear the plane too now! Oh, I say! This is exciting! George, Timmy won't bark and give us away, will he?'

'No. I've told him to be quiet,' said George. 'He won't make a sound. Listen, the plane is coming nearer!'

The noise was now loud enough for them to search the starry sky for the plane. Julian gave Dick a nudge. 'Look, you can just see it, straight over where the travellers' camp is!'

Dick managed to pick it out. 'It's very small,' he said. 'Smaller even than I thought it was last night. Look, it's coming down!'

But it wasn't. It merely swept low, and then went round in a circle, as it had done the night before. It rose a little again and then came in low once more, almost over the boys' heads.

Then something extraordinary happened. Something fell not far from Julian, something that bounced and then came to rest! It made a thud as it fell, and all four jumped. Timmy gave a startled whine.

Thud! Something else fell. Thud, thud, thud! Anne gave a squeal. 'Are they trying to bomb us or something? Julian, what are they doing?'

Thud! Thud! Julian ducked at the last two

thuds, they sounded so near. He took hold of Anne and pulled her down into the quarry, calling to Dick and George.

'Get down here, quickly! Force yourselves into the caves somewhere! We shall get hit!'

They ran across the quarry as the plane swooped round in a circle once more and then again began dropping the things that went 'thud! thud!'. Some even fell into the quarry this time. Timmy got the shock of his life when one bounced in front of his nose and rolled away. He yelped and tore after George.

Soon they were all safely squeezed into the little caves that lined the sides of the quarry. The plane swept round once more, up and then round, and the thud-thudding began again. The four could hear that some of the thuds were actually in the quarry again and they were thankful they were well sheltered.

'Well, nothing is exploding,' said Dick, thankfully. 'But what on earth is the plane dropping? And why? This is a most peculiar adventure to have.'

'It's probably a dream,' said Julian, and laughed. 'No, not even a dream could be so mad. Here we are, snuggling into sandy caves in a quarry on Mystery Moor, while a plane drops something all round us in the middle of the night! Quite mad.'

'I believe the plane's going away now,' said Dick. 'It's circled round but hasn't dropped anything. Now it's climbing, it's going away! The engine doesn't sound nearly so loud. Goodness, when we were standing out there at the edge of the quarry, I almost thought the plane would take my head off, it was so low!'

'I thought that too,' said Anne, very glad that there was to be no more swooping down and dropping dozens of unknown things. 'Is it safe to go out?'

'Oh yes,' said Julian, scrambling out of the sand. 'Come on. We shall easily hear if the plane comes back again. I want to see what it has dropped!'

In great excitement they ran to get the

parcels. The stars gave so much light on that clear night that the four did not even need a torch.

Julian picked up something first. It was a firm, flattish parcel, done up well, sewn into a canvas covering. He examined it.

'No name. Nothing,' he said. 'This is most exciting. Let's have three guesses what's inside.'

'Bacon for breakfast, I hope!' said Anne at once.

'Idiot,' said Julian, getting out a knife to slit the string threads that sewed up the canvas. 'I guess it's smuggled goods of some sort. That's what that plane was doing, I should think, flying over from France, and dropping smuggled goods in a pre-arranged place, and I suppose the travellers pick them up, and take them away, well hidden in their caravans, to deliver them somewhere. Very clever!'

'Oh Julian, is *that* the explanation?' said Anne. 'What would be in the parcels then, cigarettes?'

'No,' said Julian. 'The parcels wouldn't be so

heavy if they only contained cigarettes. There, I've slit the threads at last!'

The others crowded round to see. George took her torch out of her pocket so that they could see really well. She flashed it on.

Julian ripped off the canvas covering. Next came some strong brown paper. He ripped that off too. Then came strong cardboard, tied round with string. That was undone as well, and the cardboard fell to the ground.

'Now, what have we got?' said Julian, excited. Thin sheets of paper, dozens and dozens of them packed together. Shine your torch nearer, George.'

There was a silence as all the four craned over Julian's hands.

'Whew! I say! Gosh, do you see what they are?' said Julian, in awe. 'American money, dollar notes. But look what they are, *one hundred*-dollar notes! And my word there are scores and scores of them in this one packet.'

The four stared in amazement as Julian rifled

through the packet of notes. However much would they be worth?

'Julian, how much is a hundred-dollar note worth in our money?' asked George.

'About fifty pounds I think,' said Julian. 'Yes, just about that. Gosh, and there are scores in this one packet, and we know they dropped *dozens* of the packets too. Whatever is it all about?'

'Well, there must be thousands and thousands of dollars lying around us, here in the quarry and outside it,' said George. 'I *say*! Surely this *isn't* a dream?'

'Well, I must say it's a very *extravagant* kind of dream, if so,' said Dick. 'A dream worth thousands of pounds isn't very usual. Ju, hadn't we better get busy picking up these parcels?'

'Yes. We certainly had,' said Julian. 'I'm beginning to see it all now. The smugglers come over in a plane from France, say, having previously arranged to drop these packets in a lonely spot on this moor. The travellers are in the plot to the extent that they light the guiding lamp and pick up the parcels.'

'I see, and then they quietly pack them into their caravans, slip off the moor, and deliver them to somebody else, who pays them well for their trouble,' said Dick. 'Very smart!'

'That's about it,' said Julian. 'But I can't for the life of me see why *dollar* notes have to be smuggled here. They can be brought freely enough into the country – why *smuggle* them?'

'Stolen ones, perhaps?' said George. 'Oh well, it's quite beyond *me*. What a thing to do! No wonder the travellers didn't want us around.'

'Better buck up and collect all these parcels and clear off back to the stables with them,' said Julian, picking up one near him. 'The travellers will be after them, there's no doubt about that! We must be gone before they come.'

The four of them went about looking for the parcels. They found about sixty of them, and they made quite a heavy load.

'We'll put them somewhere safe, I think,'

said Julian. 'What about stuffing them into one
of the sand caves? I don't very well see how we
can carry them like this.'

'We could put them in the rugs and tie up the
ends and carry them like that,' said George. 'It
would be mad to leave them hidden somewhere
in this quarry. It's the first place the travellers
would search.'

'All right. We'll follow your idea,' said Julian. 'I think we've about collected all the
packets there are. Get the rugs.'

George's idea proved to be a good one. Half
the parcels were rolled into one rug, and tied
up, and half into the other.

'Good thing the rugs are nice and big,' said
Dick, tying his up strongly. 'Now I can just
about manage mine nicely on my back. You all
right, Ju?'

'Yes, come along, you girls,' said Julian.
'Follow behind us. We'll go down the railway
line. Leave everything else here. We can easily
get it another time. We *must* leave before the
travellers come.'

Timmy began to bark suddenly. 'That must mean the travellers are coming,' said Dick. 'Come on, quick! Yes, I can hear their voices – for goodness' sake, HURRY!'

## [16]

## *The terrible mist*

Yes, the travellers were certainly coming! Their dogs were with them, barking. The four children hurried out of the quarry with Timmy at their heels, quite silent.

'Those fellows may not know we were camping in the quarry,' panted Dick. 'They may just be coming to find the parcels, and while they are hunting around, we may be able to get a good start. Buck up!'

They set off to where the lines ended, near where the old engine lay half-buried. The travellers' dogs heard them and set up a yelping and howling. The travellers stopped to see what had excited them.

They spied shadows moving in the distance, the four children slipping away from the quarry. One of the men shouted loudly.

'Hey you – stop! Who are you? Stop, I say!'

But the five didn't stop. They were now stumbling between the railway lines, glad of George's torch and Anne's. The boys could not have held one for it was all they could do to hang on to the heavy-laden rugs.

'Quick, oh quick!' whispered Anne, but it was impossible to go very quickly.

'They must be catching us up,' said Julian, suddenly. 'Look round and see, George.'

George looked round. 'No, I can't see anyone,' she said. 'Julian, everywhere looks peculiar. What's happening? Julian, stop. Something strange is happening!'

Julian stopped and looked round. His eyes had been fixed on his feet, trying to see where he was going without stumbling. Anne had shone her torch down for him but it was still difficult to get along properly. Julian gazed all round, wondering what George meant.

Then he gave a gasp. 'Gosh! How strange! There's a mist come up, look. It's even blotted out the stars. No wonder it seems so jolly dark all of a sudden.'

'A mist!' said Anne, scared. 'Not that *awful* mist that sometimes covers the moor! Oh Julian, is it?'

Julian and Dick watched the swirling mist in astonishment. 'It's come from the sea,' Julian said. 'Can't you smell the salt in it? It's come just as suddenly as we've been told it comes, and look, it's getting thicker every minute!'

'What a good thing we're on the railway lines!' said George. 'What shall we do? Go on?'

Julian stood and thought. 'The travellers won't come after us in this mist,' he said. 'I've a good mind to hide this money somewhere, and then walk back to get the police. If we keep on the lines we can't go wrong. But we must be sure not to leave them, or we'll be completely lost!'

'Yes, let's do that,' said Dick, who was heartily sick already of lugging along his heavy load. 'But where do you propose to hide them, Ju? Not in the quarry! We'd have to walk through this awful mist to do that, and we'd get lost at once.'

'No. I've thought of a fine place,' said Julian, and he lowered his voice. 'Remember that old engine, fallen on its side? Well, what about stuffing these packets all the way down that great long funnel, and then stopping the top of it up with sand? I bet you anything you like that nobody would find the packets there.'

'Grand idea!' said Dick. 'The travellers will be sure we've gone off carrying the money, and they'll not hunt about for it long, once they find the dropped packets are all gone. We'll be halfway home by the time they try to catch us, if they dare to brave this mist.'

Anne and George thought Julian's idea was first-rate, a stroke of genius. 'I'd never, never have thought of the engine funnel!' said Anne.

'Now, there's no need for you two girls and Timmy to walk all the way to the engine with us,' said Julian. 'You sit down here on the lines and wait for us to come back. We shan't be long. We'll walk straight up the railway, find the engine, pack the money into the funnel, and walk back.'

'Right,' said George, squatting down. 'Bring the rugs back with you, though. It's cold now!'

Julian and Dick went off together, with Anne's torch. George kept hers. Timmy pressed close against her, astonished at the thick mist that had so suddenly swirled up and around them.

'That's right. Keep close to us and keep us warm, Tim,' said George. 'It's jolly cold now. This mist is damp!'

Julian stumbled along, keeping a look-out for the travellers. He could see nothing of them, but then, if they had been only two feet away he could not have seen anything of them in the mist! It seemed to get thicker and thicker.

I know what old Ben meant now, when he said that it had damp fingers, thought Julian, feeling little touches like fingers on his face, hands and legs as the mist wreathed itself round him.

Dick nudged him. 'Here we are,' he said.

'The lines are broken here. The engine should be just over there, a few feet away.'

They stepped cautiously away from the lines. The big gorse bush could not be seen, but it could be felt! Julian felt thorns pricking his legs, and knew he was beside it.

'Shine your torch here, Dick,' he whispered. 'That's right. There's the cab of the engine, see? Now let's circle the bush, and we'll come to the funnel.'

'Here it is,' said Dick, in a few moments. 'Look! Now then, let's do a bit of work, shoving these packets down. Gosh, what a lot of them there are! I hope the funnel will take them all.'

They spent ten minutes ramming the packets into the wide funnel. Down they went to the bottom! More and more followed and then, at last, the final one was shoved in and rammed down.

'That's the lot,' said Dick, relieved. 'Now we'll pack some sand in. Gosh, isn't this bush full of prickles! It's really spiteful!'

'The packets *almost* fill the funnel,' said Julian. 'Hardly any room for sand. Still, we can put in enough to hide the money all right. There, that's done. Now pull this gorse branch over the top of the funnel. My word, I never knew a bush so set with spines! I'm scratched to bits!'

'Can you hear anything of the travellers?' asked Dick, in a low voice, as they prepared to go back to the lines.

They listened. 'Not a thing,' said Julian. 'It's my belief they're scared of this mist, and are lying low till it clears.'

'They may be in the quarry,' said Dick. 'Waiting there in safety. Well, long may they be there! They won't get the money now!'

'Come on,' said Julian, and walked round the bush. 'It's just about here that we step out to get to the lines. Take my arm. We mustn't get separated. Did you ever see such a mist in your life? It's the thickest fog I ever knew. We can't even see our feet in the light of the torch now.'

They took a few steps and then felt about for

the rails. They couldn't feel even one. 'A bit farther, I think,' said Julian. 'No, this way.'

But they still couldn't find the railway lines. Where *were* the wretched things? A small feeling of panic came into Julian's mind. Which way should they step now, to find the rails? How had they gone wrong?

Now both boys were on hands and knees, feeling for the broken rails. 'I've got one,' said Dick. 'No, blow, it isn't. It's a bit of wood, or something. For goodness' sake, keep close to me, Ju.'

After ten minutes' search, the two boys sat back on their heels, the little torch between them.

'Somehow we've just missed those two or three correct steps from the gorse bush to the rails,' said Julian. 'Now we're done for! I don't see anything for it but to wait till the mist clears.'

'But what about the two girls?' said Dick, anxiously. 'Let's try a bit longer. Look, the mist is clearing a little there. Let's go forward and hope we'll stumble over the lines soon. If the mist does clear, we shall soon be able to get our bearings.'

So they went forward hopefully, seeing the mist clear a little in front of them, so that the torch made a longer beam for them to see by. Now and again, when their feet knocked against something hard, they felt for the rails. But they could not find even one!

'Let's shout,' said Julian, at last. So they shouted loudly. 'George! Anne! Can you hear us?'

They stood and listened. No answer.

'GEORGE!' yelled Dick. 'TIMMY!'

They thought they heard a far-off bark. 'That was Timmy!' said Julian. 'Over there!'

They stumbled along and then shouted again. But this time there was no bark at all. Not a sound came out of that dreadful mist, which had now closed tightly round them again.

'We'll be walking in it all night long,' said Julian, desperately. 'Why did we leave the girls?

Suppose this frightful fog doesn't clear by to-morrow? Sometimes it lasts for days.'

'What a horrible idea,' said Dick, lightly, sounding much more cheerful than he felt. 'I don't think we need worry about the girls, Ju. Timmy's with them and he can easily take them back to the stables across the moor, in the mist. Dogs don't mind fogs.'

Julian felt most relieved. He hadn't thought of that. 'Oh yes, I'd forgotten old Tim,' he said. 'Well, seeing that the girls will probably be all right with Timmy to guide them, let's sit down somewhere and have a rest. I'm tired out!'

'Here's a good thick bush,' said Dick. 'Let's get into the middle of it if we can, and keep the damp out of us. Thank goodness it's not a gorse bush!'

'I wish I knew if the girls had had the sense not to wait for us any longer, but to try to find their way back down the lines,' said Julian. 'I wonder where they are now?'

\*　　\*　　\*

Anne and George were no longer where Julian and Dick had left them! They had waited and waited, and then had become very anxious indeed.

'Something's happened,' said George. 'I think we ought to go and get help, Anne. We can easily follow the railway down to where we have to break off for the stable. Timmy will know, anyway. Don't you think we ought to go back and get help?'

'Yes, I do,' said Anne, getting up. 'Come on George. Gosh, this mist is worse than ever! We'll have to be careful we don't lose the lines! Even Timmy might find it hard to smell his way in this fog!'

They got up. Anne followed George and Timmy followed behind, looking puzzled. He couldn't understand this night-time wandering about at all!

Anne and George kept closely to the railway lines, walking slowly along, shining the light of the torch downwards, and following carefully.

After a time George stopped, puzzled. 'This

line's broken here,' she said. 'There's no more of it. That's funny, I don't remember it being as badly broken as this. The lines simply stop. I can't see any more.'

'Oh *George*!' said Anne, peering down. 'Do you know what we've done? We've come all the way *up* the lines again – instead of going down them, homewards! How *could* we have been so mad? Look, this is where they break off, so the old engine must be somewhere near, and the quarry!'

'Blow!' said George, quite in despair. 'What asses we are. It shows how we can lose our sense of direction in a mist like this.'

'I can't see or hear anything of the boys,' said Anne, fearfully. 'George, let's go to the quarry and wait there till daylight comes. I'm cold and tired. We can squeeze into one of those warm sand caves.'

'All right,' said George, very much down in the dumps. 'Come along, and for goodness' sake don't let's lose our way to the quarry!'

# [17]

## Prisoners together

The two girls and Timmy made their way carefully, hoping to come across the lines that led to the quarry. They were lucky. They went across the gap in the lines where once long ago the travellers had wrenched out the rails, and came to where they began again, and led to the edge of the quarry.

'Here they are!' said George, thankfully. 'Now we're all right. We've only just got to follow these and we'll be in the quarry. I hope it will be warmer than here. Brrr! This mist is terribly cold and clammy.'

'It came up so *suddenly*,' said Anne, shining her torch downwards. 'I couldn't believe my eyes when I looked round and saw it creeping up on us. I—'

She stopped suddenly. Timmy had given a

low growl. 'What's up, Tim?' whispered George. He stood quite still, his hackles up and his tail motionless. He looked steadfastly into the mist.

'Oh dear. What can be the matter now?' whispered Anne. 'I can't hear a thing, can you?'

They listened. No, there was nothing to hear at all. They went on into the quarry, thinking that Timmy might have heard a rabbit or hedgehog, and growled at it as he sometimes did.

Timmy heard a sound and ran to the side, lost in the mist at once. He suddenly yelped loudly, then there was a heavy thud, and no more sound from Timmy!

'Timmy! What's happened? Timmy, come here!' shouted George, at the top of her voice. But no Timmy came. The girls heard the sound of something heavy being dragged away, and George ran after the sound.

'Timmy! Oh Timmy, what's happened!' she cried. 'Where are you? Are you hurt?'

The mist swirled round, and she tried to beat against it with her fists, angry that she could not see. 'Tim! Tim!'

Then a pair of hands took her arms from behind and a voice said, 'Now you come with me! You were warned not to snoop about on the moor!'

George struggled violently, less concerned for herself than for Timmy.

'Where's my dog?' she cried. 'What have you done to him?'

'I knocked him on the head,' said the voice, which sounded very like Sniffer's father. 'He's all right, but he won't feel himself for a bit! You can have him back if you're sensible.'

George wasn't sensible. She kicked and fought and wriggled and struggled. It was no use. She was held in a grip like iron. She heard Anne scream once and knew that she had been caught too.

When George was too tired to struggle any more, she was led firmly out of the quarry with Anne.

'Where's my dog?' she sobbed. 'What have you done with him?'

'He's all right,' said the man behind her. 'But if you make any more fuss I'll give him another blow on the head. NOW will you be quiet.'

George was quiet at once. She was taken with Anne across the moor for what seemed like miles, but was really only the fairly short distance between the quarry and the travellers' camp.

'Are you bringing my dog?' asked George, unable to contain her fears about Timmy.

'Yes. Somebody's got him,' said her captor. 'You shall have him back safe and sound, if you do what you're told!'

George had to be content with that. What a night! The boys gone, Timmy hurt, she and Anne captured, and this horrible, wreathing mist all the time!

The mist cleared a little as they came near to the travellers' camp. The hill behind seemed to keep it off. George and Anne saw the light of a fire, and of a few lanterns here and there. More men were gathered together, waiting. Anne thought she could see Sniffer and Liz in the background but she couldn't be sure.

If only I could get hold of Sniffer, she thought. He would soon find out if Timmy is really hurt. Oh Sniffer, do come nearer if it's you!

Their captors took them to the little fire, and made both girls sit down. One of the men there exclaimed in surprise.

'But these are not those two boys! This is a boy and a girl, not as tall as the others were!'

'We're two girls,' said Anne, thinking that the men might treat George less roughly if they knew she was not a boy. 'I'm a girl and so is she.'

She got a scowl from George, but took no notice. This was not the time to pretend anything. These men were ruthless, and very angry. They thought their plans had gone wrong, all because of two boys. Perhaps when they found they had got two girls, they would let them go.

The men began to question them. 'Where are the boys then?'

'We've no idea! Lost in the mist,' said Anne. 'We all went out to go back home, and got separated, so George, I mean Georgina, and I went back to the quarry.'

'Did you hear the plane?'

'Of course!'

'Did you see or hear it dropping anything?'

'We didn't *see* anything drop, we heard it,' said Anne. George stared at her furiously. Why was Anne giving all this away? Perhaps she thought that Timmy would be given back to them if they proved helpful? George immediately changed her mind about feeling cross with Anne. If only Timmy were all right!

'Did you pick up what the plane dropped?' The man rapped out the question so sharply that Anne jumped. What should she say?

'Oh yes,' she heard herself saying. 'We picked up a few strange parcels. What was in them, do you know?'

'Never you mind,' said the man. 'What did you do with the parcels?'

George stared at Anne, wondering what she was going to say? Surely, surely she wouldn't give *that* secret away?

'I didn't do anything with them,' said Anne, in an innocent voice. 'The boys said they would hide them. So they went off into the mist with them, but they didn't come, back. So George and I went to the quarry again. That's when you caught us.'

The men talked among themselves in low voices. Then Sniffer's father turned to the girls again.

'Where did the boys hide these packets?'

'How do I know?' said Anne. 'I didn't go with them. I didn't see what they did with them.'

'Do you think they will still have got them with them?' asked the man.

'Why don't you go and *find* the boys and ask them?' said Anne. 'I haven't seen or heard of the boys since they left us and went into the mist. I don't know *what* became of them or the parcels!'

'They're probably lost somewhere on the moors,' said the old, grey-haired traveller. 'With the packets! We'll look for the boys tomorrow. They won't get home in this! We'll fetch them back here.'

'They wouldn't come,' said George. 'As soon as they saw you, they'd run. You'd never catch them. Anyway they'd get back home as soon as the mist cleared.'

'Take these girls away,' said the old traveller, sounding tired of them. 'Put them in the far cave, and tie them up.'

'Where's my dog?' shouted George, suddenly. 'You bring me my dog!'

'You haven't been very helpful,' said the old traveller. 'We'll question you again tomorrow, and if you are *more* helpful, you shall have your dog.'

Two men took the girls away from the fire and over to the hill. A large opening led into the strange hill. One of the men had a lantern and led the way, the other man walking behind.

A passage led straight into the hill. There was

sand underfoot, and it seemed to Anne as if even the walls were made of sand. How strange!

The hill was honeycombed with passages. They criss-crossed and forked like burrows in a rabbit warren. Anne wondered however the men could find their way!

They came at last to a cave that must have been right in the heart of the hill, a cave with a sandy floor, and a post that was driven deeply into the ground.

Ropes were fastened firmly to it. The two girls looked at them in dismay. Surely they were not going to be tied up like prisoners!

But they were! The ropes were fastened firmly round their waists and knotted at the back. The knots were travellers' knots, firm, tight and complicated. It would take the girls hours to unpick those, even supposing they could manage to reach right round to their backs!

'There you are,' said the men, grinning at the two angry girls. 'Maybe in the morning you will remember where those packets were put!'

'You go and get my dog,' ordered George. But they only laughed loudly and went out of the cave.

It was stuffy and hot in there. George was worried to death about Timmy, but Anne was almost too tired to think.

She fell asleep, sitting up uncomfortably with the ropes round her waist, and the knots digging into her back. George sat brooding. Timmy – where was he? Was he badly hurt? George was very miserable indeed.

She didn't go to sleep. She sat there, worrying, wide awake. She made an attempt to get at the knots behind her, but it was no use, she couldn't.

Suddenly she thought she heard a noise. Was that someone creeping up the passage to the cave? She felt frightened. Oh, if only Timmy were here!

Sniff! Sniff!

'Gracious goodness, it must be Sniffer!'

thought George, and at that moment she almost loved the dirty little traveller boy!

'Sniffer!' she called quietly, and put on her torch. Sniffer's head appeared and then his body. He was crawling quietly up the passage on all fours.

He came right into the cave, and stared at her and the sleeping Anne. 'I've sometimes been tied up here too,' he said.

'Sniffer, how is Timmy?' asked George, anxiously. 'Tell me, quickly!'

'He's all right,' said Sniffer. 'He's just got a bad cut on his head. I bathed it for him. *He's* tied up too, and he's mad about it!'

'Sniffer, listen, go and get Timmy and bring him to me,' said George, breathlessly. 'And bring me a knife too, to cut these ropes. Will you? Can you?'

'Oooh, I dunno,' said Sniffer, looking frightened. 'My father would half kill me!'

'Sniffer, is there anything you want, anything you've *always* wanted?' said George. 'I'll give it to you if you do this for me, I promise you!'

'I want a bike,' said Sniffer, surprisingly. 'And I want to live in a house, and ride my bike to school.'

'I'll see that you have what you want, Sniffer,' said George, wildly. 'Only, do, do go and get Timmy, and a knife! You got here without being seen, you can surely get back again safely with Timmy. Think of that bike!'

Sniffer thought of it. Then he nodded and disappeared down the passage as silently as he had come.

George waited and waited. Would he bring dear old Timmy to her, or would he be caught?

# [18]

# *George's trick*

George sat in the darkness of the cave, hearing Anne's peaceful breathing nearby, waiting for Sniffer to come back. She was longing to see Timmy again. Was the cut on his head *very* bad?

A thought came into her mind. She would send Timmy back to the stables with a note! He was very clever, he knew what to do when he had a note tied to his collar. Then help would come very quickly indeed. Timmy would know his way all right out of this hill, once he had been in it!

Ah, here was Sniffer coming back again. Was Timmy with him? She heard Sniffer's sniff-sniff-sniff, but no sound of Timmy. Her heart sank.

Sniffer appeared cautiously in the cave.

'I didn't dare to take Timmy,' he said. 'My father has him tied up too near to him, and I'd have woken him. But I've brought you a knife, look.'

'Thank you, Sniffer,' said George, taking the knife and putting it into her pocket. 'Listen, there's something important I'm going to do and you've got to help.'

'I'm scared,' said Sniffer. 'I'm really scared.'

'Think of that bicycle,' said George. 'A red one, perhaps with silver handles?'

Sniffer thought of it. 'All right,' he said. 'What are you going to do?'

'I'm going to write a note,' said George, feeling in her pocket for her notebook and pencil. 'And I want you to tie it on to Timmy's collar, under his chin, and set him free somehow. Will you do that? He'll run off back to the stables with the note, and then Anne and I will be rescued, and you will get the most beautiful bicycle in the world!'

'And a house to live in,' said Sniffer, at once. 'So that I can ride my bike to school?'

'All right,' said George, hoping that somehow he could have that too. 'Now, wait a
minute.'

She scribbled the note, but she had hardly
written more than a few words, when a sound
came up the passage. Someone was coughing.

'It's my father!' said Sniffer, in fright. 'Listen,
if you cut your ropes and escape, can you find
your way out from here? It's very twisty and
turny.'

'I don't know. I don't think I can!' whispered
George, in a panic.

'I'll leave patrins for you!' said Sniffer. 'Look
out for them! Now I'm going to slip into the
cave next door, and wait till my father's finished talking to you. Then I'll go back to
Timmy.'

He slipped out just in time. The lantern shone
into George's cave and Sniffer's father stood
there.

'Have you seen Sniffer?' he asked. 'I missed
him when I woke just now. If I catch him in here
I'll whip him till he squeals.'

'Sniffer? He's not here,' said George, trying to sound surprised. 'Look round the cave and see!'

The man caught sight of the notebook and pencil in George's hand. 'What's that you're writing?' he said suspiciously and took it from her.

'So you're writing for help, are you!' he said. 'And how do you think you're going to get help, I'd like to know? Who's going to take this note home for you? Sniffer?'

'No,' said George, truthfully.

The man frowned as he looked again at the note. 'Look here,' he said, 'you can write another note, to those two boys. And I'll tell you what to say.'

'No,' said George.

'Oh yes, you will,' said the man. 'I'm not going to hurt those boys. I'm just going to get back those packets from wherever they are hidden. Do you want your dog back safely?'

'Yes,' said George, with a gulp.

'Well, if you don't write this note you won't see him again,' said the man. 'Now then, take your pencil and write in that notebook of yours.'

George took up her pencil. 'This is what you must write,' said the man, frowning as he thought hard.

'Wait a minute,' said George. 'How are you going to get this note to the boys? You don't know where they are! You won't be able to find them if this mist still goes on.'

The man scratched his head and thought.

'The only way to get the note to them is to tie it on my dog's collar and send him to find them,' said George. 'If you bring him here to me I can make him understand. He always does what I tell him.'

'You mean he'll take the note to whoever you tell him to take it?' said the man, his eyes gleaming. 'Well, write it then. Say this:

' "We are prisoners. Follow Timmy and he will bring you to us and you can save us." Then sign your name, whatever it is.'

'It's Georgina,' said George, firmly. 'You go and get my dog while I write the note.'

The man turned and went. George looked after him, her eyes bright. *He* thought he was making her play a trick on Julian and Dick, to bring them here so that they could be threatened and questioned about the packets, and where they were hidden!

But *I'm* going to play a trick on him, thought George. I'm going to tell Timmy to take the note to *Henry*, and she'll be suspicious and get Captain Johnson to follow Tim back here, and that will give the travellers an *awful* shock! I expect the captain will be sensible enough to get the police as well. Aha, *I'm* playing a trick too!

In ten minutes' time Sniffer's father returned with Timmy. It was a rather subdued Timmy, with a very bad cut on his head, which really needed stitching. He pattered soberly across to George, and she flung her arms round his neck and cried into his thick hair.

'Does your head hurt you?' she said. 'I'll take you to the vet when I get back, Tim.'

'You can get back as soon as we've got those two boys here and they've told us where those packets are hidden,' said the man.

Timmy was licking George as if he would never stop, and his tail waved to and fro, to and fro. He couldn't understand what was happening at all! Why was George here? Never mind, he was with her again. He settled down on the floor with a thump and put his head on her knee.

'Write the note,' said the man, 'and tie it on to his collar, on the top, so that it can easily be seen.'

'I've written it,' said George. The traveller held out a dirty hand for it and read it.

*'We are prisoners. Follow Timmy and he will bring you to us and you can save us.*
                              GEORGINA.'

'Is that really your name, Georgina?' asked the man. George nodded. It was one of the few times she ever owned to a girl's name!

She tied the note firmly to Timmy's collar, on the top of his neck. It was quite plainly to be seen. Then she gave him a hug and spoke urgently to him.

'Go to Henry, Tim, go to HENRY. Do you understand, Timmy dear, take this note to HENRY.' She tapped the paper on his collar as he listened to her. Then she gave him a push. 'Go along. Don't stay here any longer. Go and find HENRY.'

'Hadn't you better tell him the other boy's name too?' said the man.

'Oh no, I don't want to *muddle* Timmy,' said George hastily. 'Henry, Henry, HENRY!'

'Woof,' said Timmy, and George knew that he understood. She gave him another push.

'Go, then,' she said. 'Hurry!'

Timmy gave her rather a reproachful look as if to say, 'You haven't let me stay with you very long!' Then he padded off down the passage, the note showing clearly on his collar.

'I'll bring the boys up here as soon as they come with the dog,' said the man, and he turned on his heel, and went out. George wondered if Sniffer was still about and she called him. But there was no answer. He must have slipped away down the passages back to his caravan.

Anne woke up then, and wondered where she was. George switched on her torch again and explained all that had happened.

'You should have woken me,' said Anne. 'Oh blow these ropes. They're *so* uncomfortable.'

'I've got a knife now,' said George. 'Sniffer gave it to me. Shall I cut our ropes?'

'Oh yes!' said Anne, in delight. 'But don't let's try and escape yet. It's still night-time and if that mist is about, we'll only get lost. We can pretend we're still tied up if anyone comes.'

George cut her own ropes with Sniffer's exceedingly blunt knife. Then she cut Anne's. Oh, what a relief to lie down properly, and not to have to sit up all the time and feel the knots at the back!

'Now do remember, if we hear anyone coming, we must tie the ropes loosely round us,' she said. 'We will stay here till we know it's day, and perhaps we can find out if the mist is still about, or if it's gone. If it's gone, we'll go.'

They fell asleep on the sandy floor, both glad to lie down flat. Nobody came to disturb them, and they slept on and on, tired out.

Where were the boys? Still under the bush, half-sleeping, half waking, for they were cold and uncomfortable. They hoped the girls were now safely at home. They must have gone right down the railway, and made their way back to the stables, thought Julian, every time he awoke. I do hope they are safe, and Timmy too. Thank goodness he is with them.

But Timmy wasn't with them, of course. He was padding across the misty moor all by himself, puzzled, and with a badly aching head. Why had George sent him to Henry? He didn't like Henry. He didn't think that George did, either. And yet she had sent him to find her. Very strange!

Still, George had given him his orders, and he loved her and always obeyed her. He padded over the heather and grass. He didn't bother about keeping to the railway line. He knew the way back without even thinking about it!

It was still night, though soon the dawn would come. But the mist was so thick that even the dawn would not be able to break through it. The sun would have to remain hidden behind the thick swathes of mist.

Timmy came to the stables. He paused to remember which was Henry's bedroom. Ah yes, it was upstairs, next to the room that Anne and George had had.

Timmy leapt into the kitchen through a window left open for the cat. He padded upstairs and came to Henry's room. He pushed at the door and it opened.

In he went and put his paws on her bed. 'Woof,' he said in her ear. 'Woof! Woof! Woof!'

## [19]

## *Good old Tim!*

Henry had been fast asleep and snoring. She awoke with a tremendous jump when she felt Timmy's paw on her arm and heard his sharp little bark.

'Oooh! What is it?' she said, sitting up straight in bed and fumbling for her torch. She was quite panic-stricken. She switched on the torch with trembling fingers and then saw Timmy, his big brown eyes looking at her beseechingly.

'Why, Timmy!' said Henry, in amazement. '*Timmy!* Whatever are you doing here? Have the others come back? No, they couldn't have, not in the middle of the night! Why have *you* come then, Timmy?'

'Woof,' said Timmy, trying to make her understand that he was bringing a message.

Henry put out her hand to pat his head, and suddenly caught sight of the paper tied to his collar at the back.

'What's this on your collar?' she said, and reached out for it. 'Why, it's paper. Tied on, too. It must be a message!'

She untied the piece of paper and unrolled it. She read it.

*'We are prisoners. Follow Timmy and he will bring you to us and you can save us.*
                                        GEORGINA.'

Henry was astounded. She looked at Timmy and he looked back, wagging his tail. He pawed at her arm impatiently. Henry read the note again. Then she pinched herself to make sure she was not dreaming.

'Oooh, no I'm awake all right,' she said. 'Timmy, is this note true? *Are* they prisoners? And who does "we" mean? George and Anne, or the whole four? Oh, Timmy I *do* wish you could speak!'

Timmy wished the same! He pawed energetically at Henry. She suddenly saw the cut on his head and was horrified.

'You're hurt, Timmy! Oh, you poor, poor thing. Who did that to you? You ought to have that wound seen to!'

Timmy certainly had a very outsize headache, but he couldn't bother to think about that. He gave a little whine and ran to the door and back.

'Yes, I know you want me to follow you, but I've got to *think*,' said Henry. 'If Captain Johnson was here I'd go and fetch him. But he's away for the night, Timmy. And I'm sure Mrs Johnson would have the fright of her life if I fetched her. I simply don't know what to do.'

'Woof,' said Timmy, scornfully.

'It's all very well to say "Woof" like that,' said Henry, 'but I'm not as brave as you are. I *pretend* I am, Timmy, but I'm not really. I'm afraid of following you! I'm afraid of going to find the others. I might be caught too. And there's a terrible mist, Timmy, you know.'

Henry slid out of bed, and Timmy looked suddenly hopeful. Was this silly girl going to make up her mind at last?

'Timmy, there's no grown-up here tonight except Mrs Johnson, and I really *can't* wake her,' said Henry. 'She's had such a very hard, busy day. I'm going to dress, and then get William. He's only eleven, I know, but he's very sensible.'

She dressed quickly in her riding things and then set off to William's room. He slept by himself across the landing. Henry walked in and switched on her torch.

William awoke at once. 'Who's there?' he demanded, sitting up at once. 'What do you want?'

'It's me. Henry,' said Henry. 'William, a most extraordinary thing has happened. Timmy has arrived in my room with a note on his collar. Read it!'

William took the note and read it. He was most astonished. 'Look,' he said, 'George has signed herself *Georgina*. She wouldn't do that unless things were very urgent. She never, never lets herself be called anything but George. We'll have to follow Tim and go, at once, too!'

'But I can't walk miles in a mist over the moor,' said Henry, in a panic.

'We don't need to. We'll saddle our horses and go on those,' said William, beginning to dress, and sounding very sensible indeed. 'Timmy will lead the way. You go and get the horses out. *Do* buck up, Henry. The others may be in danger. You're acting like a Henrietta!'

That made Henry cross. She went out of the room at once and down into the yard. What a pity Captain Johnson happened to be away just that night. He would have decided everything at once.

Courage came to her when she got the horses. They were surprised but quite willing to go for a night-time ride, even in this thick mist! William came up in a very short time with Timmy behind him. Timmy was delighted to have William with him. He liked him, but he was not very fond of Henry.

He ran forward, just in front of the horses, and they followed behind. Both Henry and William had excellent torches, and kept them shining downwards, so that they should not miss Timmy. He did go out of sight once or twice, but came back immediately, when he heard the horses stopping.

Over the moor they rode. They didn't follow the railway, of course. Timmy didn't need to. He knew the way perfectly!

Once he stopped and sniffed the air. What had he smelt? Henry and William had no idea, but Timmy was puzzled by what he had smelt on the misty air.

Surely he had smelt the smell of the two boys, Julian and Dick? It had come on the air for a moment or two, and Timmy was half-inclined to follow it and see if the smell was right. Then he remembered George and Anne and went on through the swirling mist.

The boys were actually not very far away when Timmy smelt them. They were still in the middle of the bush, trying to keep warm, and sleep. If only they had known that Timmy was near, with Henry and William! But they didn't.

Timmy led the way. Soon they came to the quarry, but did not see it because of the mist. They went round it, led by Timmy, and rode towards the travellers' camp. Timmy slowed down, and they took warning.

'He's getting near wherever he wants to take us,' whispered William. 'Had we better dismount and tie the horses up, do you think? Their hooves may give a warning that we are near.'

'Yes. Yes, William,' said Henry, thinking that the boy was really very sensible. They dismounted quietly and tied the horses to a nearby birch tree.

They were quite near the hill in front of which was the travellers' camp. The mist was not so thick here, and the two suddenly caught sight of a dark, shadowy caravan, outlined against a camp-fire, left burning nearby. 'We'll have to be very quiet,' whispered William. 'Timmy's brought us to the travellers' camp on the moor. I had an idea that he would. The others must be held prisoner somewhere near – be as quiet as you can.'

Timmy watched them dismount. He hung his head, panting, his tail down. His head was hurting him very much, and he felt decidedly strange and giddy. But he must get to George, he must!

He led the way to the opening in the hill. William and Henry were most astonished. They followed Timmy through the maze of passages, wondering how he knew the way so surely. But Timmy didn't falter. He only needed to go somewhere once, and after that he never forgot the way!

He was going very slowly now, and his legs felt peculiar and shaky. He wanted to lie down and put his aching head on his paws. But no, he must find George. He must find George.

George and Anne were lying in the little cave, asleep. They were uncomfortable, and the cave was hot, so they were restless, waking up every few minutes. But both were asleep when Timmy walked slowly into the cave, and flopped down beside George.

George awoke when she heard William and Henry come into the cave. She thought it might be Sniffer's father coming back, and she hastily put the ropes round her waist so that she would look as if she were still tied up. Then she heard Timmy panting, and switched on her torch eagerly.

It showed her Timmy, and Henry and William! Henry was full of amazement when she saw George and Anne with ropes round their waists. She gaped at them.

'Oh Timmy darling, you fetched help!' said George, putting her arms round his neck. 'Oh Henry, I'm *so* glad you've come. But didn't you bring Captain Johnson too?'

'No. He's away,' said Henry. 'But William's here. We rode, and Timmy guided us. What-*ever's* happened, George?'

Anne awoke just then, and couldn't believe her eyes when she saw the visitors! There was a hasty discussion, and then William spoke firmly.

'If you want to escape, you'd better come now, while the travellers' camp is asleep. Timmy can guide us out of this rabbit-warren of a hill. We'd never be able to find our way out alone. Come on!'

'Come on, Tim,' said George, shaking him gently. But poor old Timmy was feeling very peculiar. He couldn't see things properly. George's voice sounded blurred to him. His head felt as heavy as lead, and somehow his legs wouldn't carry him. The blow on his head was taking real effect now, and the hurried journey over the moor and back was making it worse.

'He's ill!' said George, in a panic. 'He can't get up! Oh Timmy, what's the matter?'

'It's that cut on his head,' said William. 'It's pretty bad, and he's worn out with coming to fetch us and running all the way back again. He can't possibly guide us back, George. We'll have to do the best we can by ourselves.'

'Oh, poor, poor Timmy!' said Anne, horrified at seeing the dog stretched out quite limp on the floor of the cave. 'George, can you carry him?'

'I think so,' said George, and she lugged him up in her arms. 'He's awfully heavy, but I think I can just manage him. Perhaps the fresh air will revive him when we get outside.'

'But George, we don't know our way out of here,' said Anne, fearfully. 'If Timmy can't lead us, we're lost! We'd end up by wandering miles and miles inside the hill and never getting out!'

'Well, we'll simply *have* to make a shot at it,' said William. 'Come on, I'll lead the way. We really MUST go!'

He went out of the cave and down a passage; the others followed, George carrying the limp Timmy. But very soon William came to a fork and stopped.

'Oh dear – do we go to the left or the right?' he wondered.

Nobody knew. George shone her torch here and there, trying to remember. The beam of light picked up something on the ground near-by.

It was two sticks, one short and one long, in the shape of a cross! George gave an exclamation.

'Look – a patrin! Left by Sniffer to show us the way out. We have to take the passage that the long stick points to! Oh, I hope that Sniffer has left patrins at every corner and every fork!'

They took the right-hand way and went on, their torches making long beams in the darkness, and at every place where they might go wrong, they saw a patrin, a message left by Sniffer to show them the right way to go.

'Another cross, we go *this* way,' said Anne.

'Here's a patrin again, we take *this* fork!' said George. And so it went on until they came safely to the entrance of the hill. How thankful they were to see the mist. At least it meant that they were in the open air!

'Now to get to the horses,' said William. 'They will each have to carry two of us at once, I'm afraid.'

And then, just as they were making their way

to where they had left the horses, the travellers' dogs began to bark the place down!

'They've heard us!' said William, desperately. 'Buck up! We'll be stopped if we don't get off at once!'

Then a voice shouted loudly. 'I can see you over there, with your torches! Stop at once! Do you hear me? STOP!'

# Excitement in the morning

The dawn was coming now. The mist was no longer full of darkness, but was white, and thinning rapidly. The four children hurried to the horses, which were stamping impatiently by the trees. George couldn't go very fast because of Timmy. He really was very heavy.

Suddenly he began to struggle. The fresh, cool air had revived him and he wanted to be set down. George put him down thankfully, and he began to bark defiantly at the travellers who were now coming out of their caravans, their dogs with them.

The four children mounted hurriedly and the horses were surprised at the double weight. William swung his horse's head round and set off with George sitting behind him. Henry took Anne. Timmy, feeling much better, ran after them, his legs no longer feeling so shaky.

The travellers ran too, shaking their fists and shouting. Sniffer's father was amazed beyond measure. Why, there were the two girls he had tied up – and that dog he had sent off to trick the other two boys on the moor.

Then who were these on horseback, and how had they found their way to the hill? How had the prisoners been able to find their way *out* of the hill, too? That was a real puzzle to Sniffer's father.

The travellers tore after the horses, but the dogs contented themselves with excited barks. Not one of them dared to go after Timmy. They were afraid of him.

The horses went off as fast as they dared in the mist, Timmy running in front. He seemed very much better, though George was afraid it was only the excitement that now kept him going. She glanced back at the travellers. They would never catch up now, thank goodness!

Somewhere behind the mist the sun was

shining. Soon it would disperse the strange fog that had come up so suddenly from the sea. She glanced down at her watch. Good gracious, could it really be almost six o'clock in the morning. It was tomorrow now!

She wondered what had happened to Julian and Dick. She thought of Sniffer gratefully, and all those patrins he had left in the hill. They would never have got out but for those. She thought of Henry and William, and gave William a sudden tight hug round the waist for coming out in the middle of the night and rescuing them!

'Where are Julian and Dick, do you suppose?' she said to William. 'Do you think they are still lost on the moor? Ought we to shout, and look for them?'

'No,' called back William over his shoulder. 'We're going straight back to the stables. They can look after themselves!'

Dick and Julian had certainly tried to look after themselves, that cold, misty night, but not very successfully. By the time that their torch showed them that it was a quarter to five by their watches, they had had enough of the bush they were in. If only they had known it, Henry and William, with Timmy, were just then riding over the moor, not a great distance from where they were!

They got out of the bush, damp and stiff. They stretched themselves and looked into the dark night, still full of mist.

'Let's walk,' said Julian. 'I can't bear keeping still in this mist. I've got my compass. If we walk due west we should surely come to the edge of the moor, not far from Milling Green.'

They set off, stumbling in the now dim light of the torch, whose battery was getting low. 'It will give out soon,' groaned Dick, giving it a shake. 'Blow the thing! It hardly gives us any light now, and we simply must keep looking at the compass.'

Julian tripped against something hard and almost fell. He snatched the torch from Dick. 'Quick, let me have it!'

He shone it on what had tripped him and gave a delighted exclamation. 'Look, it's a rail! We're on the railway line again. What a bit of luck!'

'I should *think* so!' said Dick, relieved. 'This torch is just about finished. Now, for GOOD-NESS' sake don't let's lose this railway line. Stop at once if you can't feel it with your foot.'

'To think we were so jolly near the line after all, and didn't know it!' groaned Julian. 'We could have been back at the stables ages ago. I do hope the girls got back safely and didn't alarm anyone about us. They'd know we would come back as soon as it was daylight, anyhow, if we could follow the lines!'

They stumbled in at the stables' entrance about six o'clock, tired out. Nobody was yet up, it seemed. They found the garden door open, left ajar by William and Henry, and went up to the girls' room, hoping to find them in bed.

But the beds were empty of course. They went to Henry's room, to ask her if she had heard anything of the girls, but her bed, though slept in, was empty too!

They went across the landing to William's room. '*He's* gone as well!' said Dick, in great astonishment. 'Where are they all?'

'Let's wake Captain Johnson,' said Julian, who had no idea that the captain was away for the night. So they awakened a very startled Mrs Johnson, and almost scared the life out of her, for she thought they were far away, camping on the moor!

She was even more startled when she heard their tale and realised that George and Anne were missing. 'Where *are* the girls, then!' she said, flinging on a dressing-gown. 'This is serious, Julian. They might be completely lost on the moor, or those travellers might have got them! I must telephone my husband, and the police too. Oh dear, oh dear, why did I ever let you go camping out!'

She was in the middle of telephoning, with Julian and Dick beside her, looking very anxious indeed, when the sound of horses' hooves came in the yard below.

'Now goodness me! Who's that?' said

Mrs Johnson. 'Horses! Who's riding them at this time of the morning?'

They all went to the window and looked down into the yard. Dick gave a yell that almost made Mrs Johnson fall out of the window!

'Anne! George! Look, there they are, and Timmy too. And gosh, there's Henry, and William! What is all this?'

Anne heard the yell and looked up. Tired as she was, she gave a cheerful wave and a grin. George gave a shout.

'Oh Julian! Oh Dick, you're back then! We did hope you would be. After you left us we went back up the lines the wrong way and arrived at the quarry again!'

'And the travellers took us prisoner!' yelled Anne.

'But – but – how do Henry and William come into this?' said poor Mrs Johnson, thinking she must really still be asleep. 'And what's the matter with Timmy?'

Timmy had suddenly flopped on the ground. The excitement was over, they were home, now he could put his poor aching head on his paws and sleep!

George was off her horse immediately. 'Timmy! Darling Timmy! *Brave* Timmy! Help me, William. I'll take him upstairs to my room and see to that cut.'

By this time all the other children were awake and there was such a pandemonium going on that Mrs Johnson couldn't make herself heard.

Children in dressing-gowns and without, children shouting and yelling, children pouring into the yard and asking questions; William trying to quiet the two horses which were getting very excited at all this sudden clamour; and all the cocks round about crowing their heads off! *What* an excitement!

The sun suddenly shone out brilliantly, and the last wisps of mist disappeared. 'Hurrah! That mist has gone!' shouted George. 'The sun's out. Cheer up, Timmy. We'll all be all right now!'

Timmy was half-carried, half-dragged up the stairs by William and George. George and

Mrs Johnson examined his cut head carefully, and bathed it.

'It really should have been stitched up,' said Mrs Johnson, 'but it seems to be healing already. How wicked to hit a dog like that!'

Soon there was the sound of horse's hooves again in the yard, and Captain Johnson arrived, looking very anxious. At almost the same moment a car slid in at the gates, a police car, with two policemen who had been sent to inquire about the missing girls! Mrs Johnson had forgotten to telephone again to say they had arrived.

'Oh dear, I'm so sorry to have bothered you,' said Mrs Johnson to the police sergeant. 'The girls have just arrived back, but I still don't know what has really happened. Still, they're safe, so please don't bother any more.'

'Wait!' said Julian, who was in the room, too. 'I think we *shall* need the police! Something very peculiar has been happening up on the moor.'

'Really? What's that?' said the sergeant, taking out a notebook.

'We were camping there,' said Julian. 'And a plane came over, very low, guided by a lamp set in a sandpit by the travellers.'

'A lamp set by the *travellers*!' said the sergeant, surprised. 'But why should they need to guide a plane? I suppose it landed?'

'No. It didn't,' said Julian. 'It came again the next night, and did exactly the same thing, swooping low and circling. But this time it dropped packages!'

'Oh, it did, did it?' said the sergeant, more interested. 'For the travellers to pick up, by any chance?'

'Yes,' said Julian. 'But the plane's aim wasn't very good, and the packets fell all round *us* and almost hit us. We ran for shelter, because we didn't know if there were any explosives or not!'

'Did you pick up any of the packages?' asked the sergeant. Julian nodded.

'Yes, we did, and I opened one.'

'What was in it?'

'Paper money, dollars!' said Julian. 'In one packet alone there were scores of notes and each note was for a hundred dollars, about fifty pounds a time! Thousands of pounds' worth thrown all around us!'

The sergeant looked at his companion. 'Ha! Now we know! This explains a lot that has been puzzling us, doesn't it, Wilkins?'

Wilkins, the other policeman, nodded grimly. 'It certainly does. So that's what happens! That's how the gang get the dollars over here, from that printing-press in North France. Just a nice little run in a plane!'

'But why do they throw the packets down for the *travellers* to collect?' asked Julian. 'Is it so that they can give them to someone else? Why don't they bring them openly into the country? Surely anyone can bring *dollars* here?'

'Not *forged* ones, my lad,' said the sergeant. 'These will all be forged, you mark my words. The gang have got a headquarters near London, and as soon as those packets are handed over to them by one of the travellers, they will set to work passing them off as real ones, paying hotel bills with them, buying all kinds of goods and paying for them in notes that aren't worth a penny!'

'Whew!' said Julian. 'I never thought of them being forged!'

'Oh yes. We've known of this gang for some time, but all we knew was that they had a printing-press to print the notes in North France, and that somehow the rest of the gang here, near London, received them and passed them off as real ones,' said the sergeant. 'But we didn't know how they were brought here, nor who took them to the gang near London.'

'But now we know all right!' said Wilkins. 'My word, this is a pretty scoop, Sergeant. Good kids these, finding out what we've been months trying to discover!'

'Where are these packages?' said the sergeant. 'Did you hide them? Did the travellers get them?'

'No, we hid them,' said Julian. 'But I guess

the travellers will be hunting all over the place for them today, so we'd better get on the moors quick, Sergeant.'

'Where did you hide them?' said the sergeant. 'In a safe place, I hope!'

'Oh very!' said Julian. 'I'll call my brother, Sergeant. He'll come with us. Hey, Dick! Come on in here, and you'll hear a very interesting bit of news!'

# [21]

## The end of the mystery

Mrs Johnson was amazed to hear that the police wanted Julian and Dick to go out on the moors again.

'But they're tired out!' she said. 'They need something to eat. Can't it wait?'

'I'm afraid not,' said the sergeant. 'You needn't worry, Mrs Johnson. These boys are tough!'

'Well actually I don't think that the travellers can *possibly* find the packets,' said Julian. 'So it wouldn't matter if we had a bite to eat. I'm ravenous!'

'All right,' said the big policeman, putting away his notebook. 'Have a snack and we'll go afterwards.'

Well, of course, George, Anne and Henry all wanted to go too, as soon as they heard about the proposed jaunt over the moors!

'What! Leave us out of *that*!' said George, indignantly. 'What a hope! Anne wants to come too.'

'So does Henry,' said Anne, looking at George, 'even though she didn't help to find the packages of notes.'

'Of *course* Henry must come,' said George at once, and Henry beamed. George had been very struck indeed with Henry's courage in coming with William to rescue her and Anne, and very pleased that she hadn't boasted about it! But Henry knew that William was the one mostly to praise, and she had been unexpectedly modest about the whole affair.

It was quite a large party that set off after everyone had a very good breakfast. Mrs Johnson had set to work cooking huge platefuls of bacon and egg, exclaiming every now and again when she thought of all that had happened up on the moors.

'Those travellers! And fancy that plane coming like that – dropping money all over the place! And the travellers tying up Anne and George in that hill. I never heard anything like it in my life!'

Captain Johnson went with the party too. He could hardly believe the extraordinary tale that the four had to tell, five, with old Timmy! Timmy now had a beautiful patch on his head, and was feeling extremely important. Wait till Liz saw that!

Ten people set out, including Timmy, for William had been included in the party too. He tried to guess where Julian had hidden the notes, but he couldn't, of course. Julian firmly refused to tell anyone. He wanted it to be a real surprise.

They came to the quarry at last, having walked all the way up the old railway line. Julian stood on the edge of the quarry and pointed out the travellers' camp.

'Look, they're leaving,' he said. 'I bet they were afraid we'd spread the news of their behaviour, after the girls escaped.'

Sure enough, the caravans were moving slowly away.

'Wilkins, as soon as you get back, give word to have every traveller watched if he leaves the caravans,' said the sergeant. 'One of them is sure to have arranged a meeting place to give the gang the packets dropped from the plane, and if we watch those caravans, and every traveller in them, we'll soon be able to put our hands on the gang that spends the forged notes.'

'I bet it's Sniffer's father,' said Dick. 'He's the ringleader, anyway.'

They watched the caravans move away one by one. Anne wondered about Sniffer. So did George. What had she promised him last night, if he would help them? A bicycle, and to live in a house so that he could ride it to school! Well, it wasn't likely she would ever see the little boy again, but if she did she would certainly have to keep her word!

'Now, where's this wonderful hiding-place?' asked the sergeant, as Julian turned from watching the caravans. He had tried to make out Sniffer and Liz, but the vans were too far away.

'Follow me!' said Julian, with a sudden grin, and led the way back up the lines to where they broke off. The gorse bush was there, and the old engine lay on its side as before, almost hidden.

'Whatever's that?' said the sergeant, surprised.

'It's the old Puffing Billy that used to pull the trucks of sand from the quarry,' said Dick. 'Apparently there was a quarrel long ago between the owners of the quarry and the travellers, and the travellers pulled up the lines and the engine ran off and fell over. There it's been ever since, as far as I can see!'

Julian went round to the funnel end, and bent back the prickly gorse branch that hid it. The sergeant looked on in surprise. Dick scraped the sand out of the top of the funnel and then pulled out one of the packages. He had been afraid they would not be there.

'Here you are!' he said, and tossed the packet to the sergeant. 'There are plenty more. I'll come to the one we opened in a minute – yes – here it is.'

The sergeant and Wilkins were amazed to see the packages hauled up from such a peculiar hiding-place. No wonder the travellers hadn't found them. Nobody would ever have looked down the funnel of the old engine, even if they had spotted it, half-buried as it was.

The sergeant looked at the hundred-dollar notes in the opened parcel and whistled. 'My word, this is it! We've seen these before, beautiful forgeries they are! If the gang had got rid of *this* lot, a great many people would have suffered. The money is worth nothing! How many packets did you say there were?'

'Dozens!' said Dick, and pulled more of them out of the funnel. 'Gosh, I can't reach the ones at the bottom.'

'Never mind,' said the sergeant. 'Put some sand in to hide them and I'll send a man to poke the rest out with a stick. The travellers have gone and they are the only people likely to hunt for them. This is a wonderful scoop! You kids have certainly put us on to something.'

'I'm glad,' said Julian. 'I say, we'd better collect all the things we left here yesterday, hadn't we? We went off in rather a hurry, you see, Sergeant, and left our things in the quarry.'

He and George went into the quarry to collect the things they had left there. Timmy went with them. He suddenly growled, and George stopped, her hand on his collar.

'What's up, Tim? Ju, there must be some-body here! Is it one of the travellers, do you think?'

Then Timmy stopped growling and wagged his tail. He dragged away from George's hand and ran over to one of the little caves in the sandy walls. He looked most peculiar with the patch on his head.

Out of the cave came Liz! As soon as she saw Timmy she began to turn head-over-heels as fast as she could. Timmy stared in wonder –

what a dog! How could she turn somersaults like that?

'Sniffer!' called George. 'Come on out. I know you're there!'

A pale, worried face looked out of the cave. Then Sniffer's thin, wiry little body followed, and soon he was standing in the quarry, looking scared.

'I got away from them,' he said, nodding his head towards where the travellers' camp had been. He went up to George, and gave a sniff.

'You said I could have a bike,' he said.

'I know,' said George. 'You *shall* have one, Sniffer. If you hadn't left us patrins in that hill, we'd never have escaped!'

'And you said I could live in a house and ride my bike to school,' said Sniffer urgently. 'I can't go back to my father, he'd half-kill me now. He saw those patrins I left in the hill and he chased me all over the moor for miles. But he didn't catch me. I hid.'

'We'll do the best we can for you,' promised Julian, sorry for this little waif. Sniffer sniffed.

'Where's that hanky?' demanded George. He pulled it out of his pocket, still clean and folded. He beamed at her.

'You're quite hopeless,' said George. 'Listen, if you want to go to school, you'll *have* to stop that awful sniff and use your hanky. See?'

Sniffer nodded, but put the hanky carefully back into his pocket. Then the sergeant came into the quarry and Sniffer fled at the sight of him!

'Funny little thing,' said Julian. 'Well, I should imagine that his father will be sent to prison for his share in this affair, so Sniffer will be able to get his wish and leave the caravan life to live in a house. We might be able to get him into a good home.'

'And I shall keep my word, and take some money out of my savings-bank and buy him a bicycle,' said George. 'He deserves it! Oh, do look at Liz – simply *adoring* Timmy and his patch. Don't look so important, Tim – it's only a patch on your cut!'

'Sniffer!' called Julian. 'Come back. You

needn't be afraid of this policeman. He is a friend of ours. He'll help us to choose a bicycle for you.'

The sergeant looked extremely surprised at this remark, but at any rate it brought Sniffer back at once!

'Well, we'll go back now,' said the sergeant. 'We've got what we want, and Wilkins has already started back to get somebody on to watching the travellers. Once we find out who they have to report to about this forged money we shall feel happy.'

'I hope Wilkins went along down the railway,' said Julian. 'It's so easy to get lost on this moor.'

'Yes. He had the sense to do that, after hearing how *you* got lost!' said the sergeant. 'It's wonderful up here, isn't it, so peaceful and quiet and calm.'

'Yes, you'd never think that mysteries could happen up here, would you?' said Dick. 'Old ones, and new ones! Well, I'm glad we happened to be mixed up in the newest one. It was quite an adventure!'

They all went back to the stables, to find that it was now almost lunch-time and that everyone had a large appetite to match the very large lunch that Mrs Johnson had got ready. The girls went upstairs to wash. George went into Henry's room.

'Henry,' she said, 'thanks most awfully. You're as good as a boy any day!'

'Thanks, George,' said Henry, surprised. 'You're *better* than a boy!'

Dick was passing the door and heard all this. He laughed, and stuck his head in at the door.

'I say, do let me share in these compliments!' he said. 'Just tell me I'm as good as a girl, will you?'

But all he got was a well-aimed hairbrush and a shoe, and he fled away, laughing.

Anne gazed out of her bedroom window over the moor. It looked so peaceful and serene under the April sun. No mystery about it now!

'All the same, it's a good name for you,' said Anne. 'You're full of mystery and adventure, and your last adventure waited for *us* to come and share it. I really think I'd call this adventure "Five Go To Mystery Moor".'

It's a good name, Anne. We'll call it that too!